UPON AN OLD
WALL DREAMING

Books by Ruskin Bond

Fiction
The Room on the Roof & Vagrants in the Valley
The Night Train at Deoli and Other Stories
Time Stops at Shamli and Other Stories
Our Trees Still Grow in Dehra
A Season of Ghosts
When Darkness Falls and Other Stories
A Flight of Pigeons
Delhi is Not Far
A Face in the Dark and Other Hauntings
The Sensualist
A Handful of Nuts
Maharani
Secrets
Tales of Fosterganj
A Gathering of Friends

Non-fiction
Rain in the Mountains
Scenes from a Writer's Life
A Book of Simple Living
Love Among the Bookshelves
Landour Days
Notes from a Small Room
The India I Love

Anthologies
Classic Ruskin Bond: Complete and Unabridged
Classic Ruskin Bond Volume 2: The Memoirs
Dust on the Mountain: Collected Stories
The Best of Ruskin Bond
Friends in Small Places
Indian Ghost Stories (ed.)
Indian Railway Stories (ed.)
Ghost Stories from the Raj
Tales of the Open Road
Ruskin Bond's Book of Nature
Ruskin Bond's Book of Humour
A Town Called Dehra
The Writer On the Hill

Poetry
Ruskin Bond's Book of Verse
Hip-Hop Nature Boy & Other Poems

UPON AN OLD WALL DREAMING

MORE OF MY FAVOURITE STORIES AND SKETCHES

RUSKIN BOND

foreword by
DAVID DAVIDAR

ALEPH

ALEPH BOOK COMPANY
An independent publishing firm
promoted by *Rupa Publications India*

Published in India in 2016 by
Aleph Book Company
7/16 Ansari Road, Daryaganj
New Delhi 110 002

Copyright © Ruskin Bond 2016

All rights reserved.

The author has asserted his moral rights.

The acknowledgements on Page 188 are an extension of the copyright page.

In the works of fiction in this book, names, characters, places and incidents are either the product of the author's imagination or are used fictitiously and any resemblance to any actual persons, living or dead, events or locales is entirely coincidental.

No part of this publication may be reproduced, transmitted, or stored in a retrieval system, in any form or by any means, without permission in writing from Aleph Book Company.

ISBN: 978-93-84067-47-2

5 7 9 10 8 6 4

Printed in India

This book is sold subject to the condition that it shall not, by way of trade or otherwise, be lent, resold, hired out, or otherwise circulated without the publisher's prior consent in any form of binding or cover other than that in which it is published.

For the lonely…

CONTENTS

Foreword: Words of Stone and Light   ix
Introduction: Becoming a Writer   xiii

FICTION
Bus Stop, Pipalnagar   3
A Face in the Dark   29
The Skull   31
My Father's Trees in Dehra   37
A Case for Inspector Lal   48
The Thief's Story   56
The Fight   60
Fairy Glen Palace   67
The Last Tiger   77
Tiger in the Cemetery   103
Mrs Roberts   110

NON-FICTION
Life at My Own Pace   117
A Good Philosophy   128
Great Trees of Garhwal   131
A Night Walk Home   136
A Fright in the Night   139
Birdsong in the Hills   142
Once upon a Mountain Time   148
Upon an Old Wall Dreaming   178

Stories to Tell	181
And Suddenly it's Summer	184
Epilogue: Time, You Old Gypsy Man	186
Acknowledgements	188

FOREWORD

Words of Stone and Light

I began writing this short note of appreciation about Ruskin Bond's extraordinary fiction and non-fiction in a room with a view of high mountains. Looking out at those tremendous mile-high fastnesses of rock and snow I began to better understand the inspiration for his finest work, and where it drew its power from. In the book, Ruskin tells us about the importance of the room with a view of the Himalayas where he writes: 'When I'm in my room, the stories and sketches and poems come floating in from the magic mountains that surround me, and appear on the page without much effort on my part.'

His best stories bear the stamp of the Indian mountains he has spent most of his life amongst, not just in terms of the setting and the people of these high places who are some of the most distinctive characters to be encountered in contemporary fiction, but in the deceptive simplicity of the plots, the clarity of the prose, the unhurried pace of the narrative, and an air of timelessness that permeates his best creations, whether they are people or places. This timeless quality is perhaps the most memorable aspect of Ruskin's fiction, and it is this characteristic that puts me in mind of the great mountains that inspired them. Words of stone and light that will endure.

This book is a successor to *A Gathering of Friends*, the first collection of the author's own favourites among all the stories he has ever published. To everyone's surprise and delight, that book sold out within weeks of publication, although there are dozens of collections of Ruskin's fiction and non-fiction in print. The reason for the book's success could probably be ascribed to the fact that the stories were chosen by the author. Few writers have as fervent a following as Ruskin Bond, and it probably gave his existing fans fresh insights into the stories as well as an opportunity to reread them, while new readers would have viewed it as the perfect introduction to the author's oeuvre.

Whatever the causes of the popularity of *A Gathering of Friends*, it gave us reason enough to ask Ruskin to put together a second collection of the stories, especially as there hadn't been room in the first book to accommodate all the great pieces of fiction he had thought deserved inclusion.

Upon an Old Wall Dreaming contains twenty-one pieces, of which approximately half are fiction. Some of my favourite Bond stories feature in this collection—among them, 'Bus Stop, Pipalnagar', a brilliant evocation of life in a small town in the northern Indian plains, and the very moving 'My Father's Trees in Dehra', a poignant tale of family, loss and remembrance. There are classic stories of horror and mystery such as 'A Face in the Dark', 'A Case for Inspector Lal' and 'The Thief's Story'. But in a departure from its predecessor, this book contains stories that have never been published in book form before, such as 'Mrs Roberts'. Even better, stories like 'The Skull' have never been published before.

The non-fiction in the book is just as strong as the fiction. A lot of it is reminiscent of the great British and American nature writers of the nineteenth and twentieth centuries—especially those such as Izaak Walton, Ralph Waldo Emerson, and the author's namesake, John Ruskin, who wrote brilliantly about nature and life in the country. But there are essays, too, of a reflective bent such as 'Life at My Own Pace', 'A Good Philosophy' and the brilliant 'Upon an Old Wall Dreaming' which gives this book its title. In our age of anxiety, these essays are guaranteed to have a calming and uplifting effect on anyone who cares to sample them. What makes this collection truly special, however, are a few essays such as 'And Suddenly it's Summer', and 'Time, You Old Gypsy Man' which have never been published before. In the latter essay, which ends the book, Ruskin writes, in a philosophical vein, 'As I sit here, watching the clouds go by, I think of all the hundreds of poems and stories that I have put to paper, and whether it matters if not even one of them survives my passing.' It isn't something he should worry about, for on the evidence of the past sixty years and more (which is how long he has been writing), his work will be read and remembered for as long as there are readers of good literature.

D. D.

INTRODUCTION

Becoming a Writer

As a novelist and storyteller I have always drawn upon my memories of places that I have known and lived in over the years. More than most writers, perhaps, I find myself drawing inspiration from the past—my childhood, adolescence, youth, early manhood...

It is over sixty years since I wrote my first novel, *The Room on the Roof*, the story of a sixteen-year-old on a journey of self-discovery in small-town India—chiefly Dehradun, 1950.

But for my early inspiration I must go back to the very beginning, to the small princely state of Jamnagar, tucked away in the Gulf of Kutch, in pre-independence India. Here my father started a small palace school for the girls in the royal household, and I learnt to read and write along with them. I was there till the age of six, and I still treasure vivid memories of beautiful palaces, pavilions and lakes, spacious lawns, a little port, sandy beaches—some of these landmarks preserved for me in photographs taken by my father. An old palace with pretty windows of coloured glass remained fixed in my memory and many years later gave me the story, *The Room of Many Colours*, which also inspired the most memorable episode in a TV serial called *Ek Tha Rusty*, in which that wonderful old thespian, Zora Sehgal, excelled in the role of an eccentric, albeit fictional, Rani.

The first book that I read by myself was *Alice's Adventures in Wonderland*, and it might well have been set in the palace gardens—rose bushes, privet hedges and croquet lawns all at hand! This fairy-tale world disappeared from my life forever when World War II broke out and my father joined the Royal Air Force.

I spent a memorable year and a half with him in New Delhi, then still a very new city—just the capital area and Connaught Place with its gleaming new shops and restaurants and cinemas. We had to walk through scrub jungle to get to Humayun's Tomb; take a tonga to get to the railway station at the other end of Old Delhi; keep cool with table fans and khas-khas matting well-soaked by the bhisti who came round at regular intervals. I saw Laurel and Hardy films and devoured milkshakes at the Keventers Milk Bar, even as the Quit India Movement gathered momentum.

Suddenly, I was seven years old and yet to go to a proper school. I would have been quite happy never to go to school, but my father took me to Simla (now Shimla) and put me in Bishop Cotton's where I immediately received a double promotion, having benefited from those early lessons in Jamnagar.

The best thing about Simla was the mountain railway, the best thing about school was the library. I can't say that school life inspired much of my writing, although that well-stocked library did give me a solid grounding in the classics and the literature of the time.

I was barely ten when I received news of my father's death, and my life was turned upside down for some time. I had to adjust to my stepfather's Punjabi home in Dehradun, and this took a little doing, as his main interests were shikar and second-hand cars. But Dehradun, at that time, was a pretty little town of some 40,000 inhabitants; today, it is a state capital with a population exceeding ten lakhs. The litchi gardens have given way to blocks of flats. But the old Dehra, with its country lanes, little canals, and rolling hills, found its way into many of my stories.

When I was seventeen, I was shipped off to the UK to 'better my prospects', as my mother put it. I spent two years in the Channel Islands and three in London. Out of a longing for India and the friends I had made in Dehra came my first novel, *The Room on the Roof*, featuring the life and loves of 'Rusty', my alter ego. Two years and two drafts later it found a publisher—André Deutsch. In those days the standard advance was just £50—but it was enough to bring me back to India.

In the 1950s, everyone travelled by sea, the air services were still in their infancy. A passenger liner took about three weeks from Southampton to Bombay (now Mumbai), stopping for a day or two at Gibraltar, Port Said, Aden (now Yemen), and Karachi.

Arriving at Ballard Pier, Bombay, I still had £10 with me—my entire capital, my only asset being my portable typewriter—and a couple of days later I got off the train at Dehra's small railway station and embarked on the hazardous journey of a freelance writer.

Railway stations! Trains! Platforms, with hundreds of people in transit. As long as there were trains I would never run out of stories.

Back then trains still used steam engines, and there was a certain romance attached to train journeys, a romance that was captured by Rudyard Kipling in *Kim* and many of his short stories. Wheeler's had just opened their chain of railway bookstalls, and many of Kipling's early stories (written in the 1880s when he was a journalist with the *Civil and Military Gazette*) were published by Wheeler's Indian Railway Library—collectors' items today.

I did not have Wheeler's or *The Gazette*, but I had *Sainik Samachar*, *Sport and Pastime*, *Shankar's Weekly*, *The Leader* (of Allahabad), *The Statesman*, the *Illustrated Weekly of India* and a host of other periodicals, all willing to pay a budding young writer anything from ₹25 to ₹50 for a short story. I wrote for anyone who would publish my stuff, and I had great fun eking out a living for a couple of years.

If I ran out of ideas, I had only to spend an evening at a railway station and I would come up with a story. Ambala Junction gave me 'The Woman on Platform 8', the Kalka-Simla Railway gave me 'The Tunnel'; a small, wayside halt on the fringe of the Shivalik forests gave me 'The Night Train at Deoli'.

Those small cheques enabled me to live off dhaba food, but what I needed was home cooking, so I ended up in Delhi where my mother was now living; and there I looked for inspiration in tombs and monuments and the ever-expanding city, but did not find it, and my productivity dropped. But there was that excursion to Shahjahanpur, my father's birthplace, where the old cantonment hadn't changed since 1854—providing me with the background for *A Flight of Pigeons*, the Mutiny (of 1857) story that was later made into a film called *Junoon*. by Shyam Benegal. It had been recommended to him by that legendary Urdu writer, Ismat Chughtai, who also played a small role in the film.

Escape from Delhi had become a priority for me. I felt drawn to the hills, the hills above Dehra. On the outskirts of Mussoorie I found a small cottage, tucked away in a hollow of the hills and surrounded by oak and maple trees. The rent was nominal. In 1960s' Mussoorie you could get a house for practically nothing; today, rents and prices are phenomenal.

My forty-five years in Mussoorie are an epic in themselves, and have already filled several books. I do go away sometimes— to Delhi, Orissa, Rajasthan, here and there—but I always return in some haste to my small study with its window looking out upon the mountains and the valley. Every writer needs a window. Preferably two.

Is the house, the room, the situation, important for a writer? A good wordsmith should be able to work anywhere—in a moving train, in a hotel room, on board a ship in a typhoon, or under an erupting volcano. But the room you live in, day after day and night unto night, is all important. And when I'm in my room, the stories and sketches and poems come floating in from the magic mountains that surround me, and appear on the page without much effort on my part.

Ruskin Bond
20 December 2015

FICTION

BUS STOP, PIPALNAGAR

I

My balcony was my window on the world.

The room itself had only one window, a square hole in the wall crossed by two iron bars. The view from it was rather restricted. If I craned my neck sideways, and put my nose to the bars, I could see the end of the building. Below was a narrow courtyard where children played. Across the courtyard, on a level with my room, were three separate windows belonging to three separate rooms, each window barred in the same way, with iron bars. During the day it was difficult to see into these rooms. The harsh, cruel sunlight filled the courtyard, making the windows patches of darkness.

My room was very small. I had paced about in it so often that I knew its exact measurements. My foot, from heel to toe, was eleven inches long. That made my room just over fifteen feet in length; for, when I measured the last foot, my toes turned up against the wall. It wasn't more than eight feet broad, which meant that two people was the most it could comfortably accommodate. I was the only tenant but at times I had put up at least three friends—two on the floor, two on the bed. The plaster had been peeling off the walls and in addition the greasy stains and patches were difficult to hide, though I covered the worst ones with pictures cut out from magazines—Waheeda Rehman, the Indian actress, successfully blotted out one big patch and a recent Mr Universe displayed his muscles from the opposite wall. The biggest stain was all but concealed by a calendar that showed Ganesh, the elephant-headed god, whose blessings were vital to all good beginnings.

My belongings were few. A shelf on the wall supported an untidy pile of paperbacks, and a small table in one corner of the room supported the solid weight of my rejected manuscripts and an ancient typewriter which I had obtained on hire.

I was eighteen years old and a writer.

Such a combination would be disastrous enough anywhere, but in India it was doubly so; for there were not many papers to write for and payments were small. In addition, I was very inexperienced and though what I wrote came from the heart, only a fraction touched the hearts of editors. Nevertheless, I persevered and was able to earn about a hundred rupees a month, barely enough to keep body, soul and typewriter together. There wasn't much else I could do. Without that passport to a job—a university degree—I had no alternative but to accept the classification of 'self-employed'—which was impressive as it included doctors, lawyers, property dealers, and grain merchants, most of whom earned well over a thousand rupees a month.

'Haven't you realized that India is bursting with young people trying to pass exams?' asked a journalist friend. 'It's a desperate matter, this race for academic qualifications. Everyone wants to pass his exam the easy way, without reading too many books or attending more than half- a- dozen lectures. That's where a smart fellow like you comes in! Why would students wade through five volumes of political history when they can buy a few model-answer papers at any bookstall? They are helpful, these guess-papers. You can write them quickly and flood the market. They'll sell like hot cakes!'

'Who eats hot cakes here?'

'Well, then, hot chapattis.'

'I'll think about it,' I said; but the idea repelled me. If I was going to misguide students, I would rather do it by writing second-rate detective stories than by providing them with readymade answer papers. Besides, I thought it would bore me.

II

The string of the cot needed tightening. The dip in the middle of the bed was so bad that I woke up in the morning with a stiff back. But I was hopeless at tightening bed-strings and would have to wait until one of the boys from the tea shop paid me a visit. I was too tall for the cot, anyway, and if my feet didn't stick out at one end, my head lolled over the other.

Under the cot was my tin trunk. Apart from my clothes, it contained notebooks, diaries, photographs, scrapbooks, and other odds and ends that form a part of a writer's existence.

I did not live entirely alone. During cold or rainy weather, the boys from the tea shop, who normally slept on the pavement, crowded into the room. Apart from them, there were lizards on the walls and ceilings—friends these—and a large rat—definitely an enemy—who got in and out of the window and who sometimes carried away manuscripts and clothing.

June nights were the most uncomfortable. Mosquitoes emerged from all the ditches, gullies and ponds, to swarm over Pipalnagar. Bugs, finding it uncomfortable inside the woodwork of the cot, scrambled out at night and found their way under the sheet. The lizards wandered listlessly over the walls, impatient for the monsoon rains, when they would be able to feast off thousands of insects.

Everyone in Pipalnagar was waiting for the cool, quenching relief of the monsoon.

III

I woke every morning at five as soon as the first bus moved out of the shed, situated only twenty or thirty yards down the road. I dressed, went down to the tea shop for a glass of hot tea and some buttered toast, and then visited Deep Chand the barber, in his shop.

At eighteen, I shaved about three times a week. Sometimes I shaved myself. But often, when I felt lazy, Deep Chand shaved me, at the special concessional rate of two annas.

'Give my head a good massage, Deep Chand,' I said. 'My brain is not functioning these days. In my latest story there are three murders, but it is boring just the same.'

'You must write a good book,' said Deep Chand beginning the ritual of the head massage, his fingers squeezing my temples and tugging at my hair-roots. 'Then you can make some money and clear out of Pipalnagar. Delhi is the place to go! Why, I know a man who arrived in Delhi in 1947 with nothing but the clothes he wore and a few rupees. He began by selling thirsty travellers glasses of cold water at the railway station, then he opened a small tea shop; now he has two big restaurants and lives in a house as large as the prime minister's!'

Nobody intended to live in Pipalnagar forever. Delhi was the city most aspired to but as it was 200 miles away, few could afford to travel there.

Deep Chand would have shifted his trade to another town if he had had the capital. In Pipalnagar his main customers were small shopkeepers, factory workers and labourers from the railway station. 'Here I can charge only six annas for a haircut,' he lamented. 'In Delhi I could charge a rupee.'

IV

I was walking in the wheat fields beyond the railway tracks when I noticed a boy lying across the footpath, his head and shoulders hidden by wheat plants. I walked faster, and when I came near I saw that the boy's legs were twitching. He seemed to be having some kind of fit. The boy's face was white his legs kept moving and his hands fluttered restlessly among the wheat stalks.

'What's the matter?' I said, kneeling down beside him but he was still unconscious.

I ran down the path to a Persian well, and dipping the end of my shirt in a shallow trough of water, soaked it well before returning to the boy. As I sponged his face the twitching ceased, and though he still breathed heavily, his face was calm and his hands still. He opened his eyes and stared at me, but he didn't really see me.

'You have bitten your tongue,' I said wiping a little blood from the corner of his mouth. 'Don't worry. I'll stay here with you until you are all right.'

The boy raised himself and, resting his chin on his knees he passed his arms around his drawn-up legs.

'I'm all right now,' he said.

'What happened?' I asked sitting, down beside him.

'Oh, it is nothing, it often happens. I don't know why. I cannot control it.'

'Have you been to a doctor?'

'Yes, when the fits first started, I went to the hospital. They gave me some pills that I had to take every day. But the pills made me so tired and sleepy that I couldn't work properly. So I stopped taking them. Now this happens once or twice a week. What does it matter? I'm all right when it's over and I do not feel anything when it happens.'

He got to his feet, dusting his clothes and smiling at me. He was a slim boy, long-limbed and bony. There was a little fluff on his cheeks and the promise of a moustache. He told me his name was Suraj, that he went to a night school in the city, and that he hoped to finish his high school exams in a few months' time. He was studying hard, he said, and if he passed he hoped to get a scholarship to a good college. If he failed, there was only the prospect of continuing in Pipalnagar.

I noticed a small tray of merchandise lying on the ground. It contained combs and buttons and little bottles of perfume. The tray was made to hang at Suraj's waist, supported by straps that went around his shoulders. All day he walked about Pipalnagar, sometimes covering ten or fifteen miles, selling odds and ends to people at their houses. He averaged about two rupees a day, which was enough for his food and other necessities; he managed to save about ten rupees a month for his school fees. He ate irregularly at little tea shops, at the stall near the bus stop, under the shady jamun and mango trees. When the jamun fruit was ripe, he would sit on a tree, sucking the sour fruit until his lips were stained purple. There was a small, nagging fear that he might get a fit while sitting on the tree and fall off, but the temptation to eat jamun was greater than his fear.

All this he told me while we walked through the fields towards the bazaar.

'Where do you live?' I asked. 'I'll walk home with you.'

'I don't live anywhere,' said Suraj. 'My home is not in Pipalnagar. Sometimes I sleep at the temple or at the railway station. In the summer months I sleep on the grass of the municipal park.'

'Well, wherever it is you stay, let me come with you.'

We walked together into the town, and parted near the bus stop. I returned to my room, and tried to do some writing while Suraj went into the bazaar to try selling his wares. We had agreed to meet each other again. I realized that Suraj was an epileptic, but there was nothing unusual about him being an orphan and a refugee. I liked his positive attitude to life. Most people in Pipalnagar were resigned to their circumstances, but he was ambitious. I also liked his gentleness, his quiet voice, and the smile that flickered across his face regardless of whether he was sad or happy.

V

The temperature had touched forty-three degrees Celsius, and the small streets of Pipalnagar were empty. To walk barefoot on the scorching pavements was possible only for labourers, whose feet had developed several hard layers of protective skin; and now even these hardy men lay stretched out in the shade provided by trees and buildings.

I hadn't written anything in two weeks, and though one or two small payments were due from a Delhi newspaper, I could think of no substantial amount that was likely to come my way in the near future. I decided that I would dash off a couple of articles that same night, and post them the following morning.

Having made this comforting decision, I lay down on the floor in preference to the cot. I liked the touch of things, the touch of a cool floor on a hot day; the touch of earth-soft, grassy grass was good, especially dew-drenched grass. Wet earth was soft, sensuous, as was splashing through puddles and streams.

I slept, and dreamt of a cool clear stream in a forest glade, where I bathed in gay abandon. A little further downstream was another bather. I hailed him, expecting to see Suraj but when the bather turned I found that it was my landlord's pot-bellied rent collector, holding an accounts ledger in his hands. This woke me up, and for the remainder of the day I worked feverishly at my articles.

Next morning, when I opened the door, I found Suraj asleep at the top of the steps. His tray lay at the bottom of the steps. He woke up as soon as I touched his shoulder.

'Have you been sleeping here all night?' I asked. 'Why didn't you come in?'

'It was very late,' said Suraj. 'I didn't want to disturb you.'

'Someone could have stolen your things while you were asleep.'

'Oh, I sleep quite lightly. Besides I have nothing of great value. But I came here to ask you a favour.'

'You need money?'

He laughed. 'Do all your friends mean money when they ask for favours? No, I want you to take your meal with me tonight.'

'But where? You have no place of your own and it would be too expensive in a restaurant.'

'In your room,' said Suraj. 'I shall bring the meat and vegetables and cook them here. Do you have a cooker?'

'I think so,' I said, scratching my head in some perplexity. 'I will have to look for it.'

Suraj brought a chicken for dinner—a luxury, one to be indulged in only two or three times a year. He had bought the bird for seven rupees, which was cheap. We spiced it and roasted it on a spit.

'I wish we could do this more often,' I said, as I dug my teeth into the soft flesh of a second chicken leg.

'We could do it at least once a month if we worked hard,' said Suraj.

'You know how to work. You work from morning to evening and then you work again.'

'But you are a writer. That is different. You have to wait for the right moment.'

I laughed. 'Moods and moments are for geniuses. No, it's really a matter of working hard, and I'm just plain lazy, to tell you the truth.'

'Perhaps you are writing the wrong things.'

'Perhaps, I wish I could do something else. Even if I repaired bicycle tyres, I'd make more money!'

'Then why don't you repair bicycle tyres?'

'Oh, I would rather be a bad writer than a good repairer of cycle tyres.' I brightened up, 'I could go into business, though. Do you know I once owned a vegetable stall?'

'Wonderful! When was that?'

'A couple of months ago. But it failed after two days.'

'Then you are not good at business. Let us think of something else.'

'I can tell fortunes with cards.'

'There are already too many fortune tellers in Pipalnagar.'

'Then we won't talk of fortunes. And you must sleep here tonight. It is better than sleeping on the roadside.'

VI

At noon when the shadows shifted and crossed the road, a band of children rushed down the empty street, shouting and waving their satchels. They had been at their desks from early morning, and now, despite the hot sun, they would have their fling while their elders slept on string charpoys beneath leafy neem trees.

On the soft sand near the riverbed, boys wrestled or played leapfrog. At alley corners, where tall buildings shaded narrow passages, the favourite game was gulli-danda. The gulli—a small piece of wood, about four inches long sharpened to a point at each end—is struck with the danda—a short, stout stick. A player is allowed three hits, and his score is the distance, in danda lengths, of his hits of the gulli. Boys who were experts at the game sent the gulli flying far down the road—sometimes into a shop or through a windowpane, which resulted in confusion, loud invective, and a dash for cover.

A game for both children and young men was kabaddi. This is a game that calls for good breath control and much agility. It is also known in different parts of India as hootoo-too, kho-kho and atya patya. Ramu, Deep Chand's younger brother, excelled at this game. He was the Pipalnagar kabaddi champion.

The game is played by two teams, consisting of eight or nine members each, who face each other across a dividing line. Each side in turn sends out one of its players into the opponent's area. This person has to keep on saying 'kabaddi, kabaddi' very fast and without taking a second breath. If he returns to his side after touching an opponent, that opponent is 'dead' and out of the game. If however, he is caught and cannot struggle back to his side while still holding his breath, he is 'dead'.

Ramu, who was also a good wrestler, knew all the kabaddi

holds, and was particularly good at capturing opponents. He had vitality and confidence, rare things in Pipalnagar. He wanted to go into the army after finishing school, a happy choice I thought.

VII

Suraj did not know if his parents were dead or alive. He had literally lost them when he was six. His father had been a farmer, a dark unfathomable man who spoke little, thought perhaps even less and was vaguely aware he had a son—a weak boy given to introspection and dawdling at the riverbank when he should have been helping in the fields.

Suraj's mother had been a subdued, silent woman, frail and consumptive. Her husband seemed to expect that she would not live long, but Suraj did not know if she was living or dead. He had lost his parents at Amritsar railway station in the days of Partition, when trains coming across the border from Pakistan disgorged themselves of thousands of refugees or pulled into the station half-empty, drenched with blood and littered with corpses.

Suraj and his parents had been lucky to escape one of these massacres. Had they travelled on an earlier train (which they had tried desperately to catch), they might have been killed. Suraj was clinging to his mother's sari while she tried to keep up with her husband who was elbowing his way through the frightened bewildered throng of refugees. Suraj collided with a burly Sikh and lost his grip on the sari. The Sikh had a long curved sword at his waist, and Suraj stared up at him in awe and fascination—at the man's long hair, which had fallen loose, at his wild black beard, and at the bloodstains on his white shirt. The Sikh pushed him aside and when Suraj looked around for his mother, she was not to be seen. She was hidden from him by a mass of restless bodies, all pushing in different directions. He could hear her calling his name and he tried to force his way through the crowd in the direction of her voice, but he was carried on the other way.

At night, when the platform emptied, he was still searching for his mother. Eventually, the police came and took him away. They looked for his parents but without success, and finally they sent him to a home for orphans. Many children lost their parents at about the same time.

Suraj stayed at the orphanage for two years and when he was eight, and felt himself a man, he ran away. He worked for some time as a helper in a tea shop; but when he started having epileptic fits the shopkeepers asked him to leave, and the boy found himself on the streets, begging for a living. He begged for a year, moving from one town to the next and ended up finally in Pipalnagar. By then he was twelve and really too old to beg, but he had saved some money, and with it he bought a small stock of combs, buttons, cheap perfumes and bangles, and, converting himself into a mobile shop, went from door to door selling his wares.

Pipalnagar is a small town and there was no house which Suraj hadn't visited. Everyone knew him; some had offered him food and drink; and the children liked him because he often played on a small flute when he went on his rounds.

VIII

Suraj came to see me quite often and, when he stayed late, he slept in my room, curling up on the floor and sleeping fitfully. He would always leave early in the morning before I could get him anything to eat.

'Should I go to Delhi, Suraj?' I asked him one evening.

'Why not? In Delhi, there are many ways of making money.'

'And spending it too. Why don't you come with me?'

'After my exams, perhaps. Not now.'

'Well, I can wait. I don't want to live alone in a big city.'

'In the meantime, write your book.'

'All right, I will try.'

We decided we could try to save a little money from Suraj's earnings and my own occasional payments from newspapers and magazines. Even if we were to give Delhi only a few days' trial, we would need money to live on. We managed to put away twenty rupees one week, but withdrew it the next when a friend, Pitamber, asked for a loan to repair his cycle rickshaw. He returned the money in three instalments but we could not save any of it. Pitamber and Deep Chand also had plans of going to Delhi. Pitamber wanted to own his own cycle rickshaw; Deep Chand dreamt of a swanky barber shop in the capital.

One day Suraj and I hired bicycles and rode out of Pipalnagar. It was a hot, sunny morning and we were perspiring after we had gone two miles, but a fresh wind sprang up suddenly, and we could smell the rain in the air though there were no clouds to be seen.

'Let us go where there are no people at all,' said Suraj. 'I am a little tired of people. I see too many of them all day.'

We got down from our cycles and, pushing them off the road, took a path through a paddy field and then one through a field of young maize, and in the distance we saw a tree, a crooked tree, growing beside a well. I do not even today know the name of that tree. I had never seen its kind before. It had a crooked trunk, crooked branches and it was clothed in thick, broad, crooked leaves, like the leaves on which food is served in bazaars.

In the trunk of the tree was a large hole and when I sat my cycle down with a crash, two green parrots flew out of the hole, and went dipping and swerving across the fields.

There was grass around the well, cropped short by grazing cattle, so we sat in the shade of the crooked tree and Suraj untied the red cloth in which we brought food. We ate our bread and vegetable curry, and meanwhile the parrots returned to the tree.

'Let us come here every week,' said Suraj, stretching himself out on the grass. It was a drowsy day, the air was humid and he soon fell asleep. I was aware of different sensations. I heard a cricket singing in the tree; the cooing of pigeons which lived in the walls of the old well; the soft breathing of Suraj; a rustling in the leaves of the tree; the distant drone of the bees. I smelt the grass and the old bricks around the well, and the promise of rain.

When I opened my eyes, I saw dark clouds on the horizon. Suraj was still sleeping with his arms thrown across his face to keep the glare out of his eyes. As I was thirsty, I went to the well and, putting my shoulders to it, turned the wheel very slowly, walking around the well four times, while cool clean water gushed out over the stones and along the channel to the fields. I drank from one of the trays, and the water tasted sweet; the deeper the wells, the sweeter the water. Suraj was sitting up now, looking at the sky.

'It's going to rain,' he said.

We pushed our cycles back to the main road and began riding homewards. We were a mile out of Pipalnagar when it began to rain. A lashing wind swept the rain across our faces, but we exulted in it and sang at the top of our voices until we reached the bus stop. Leaving the cycles at the hire shop, we ran up the rickety, swaying steps to my room.

In the evening, as the bazaar was lighting up, the rain stopped. We went to sleep quite early, but at midnight I was woken by the moon shining full in my face—a full moon, shedding its light all over Pipalnagar, peeping and prying into every home, washing the empty streets, silvering the corrugated tin roofs.

IX

The lizards hung listlessly on the walls and ceilings, waiting for the monsoon rains, which bring out all the insects from their cracks and crannies.

One day, clouds loomed up on the horizon, growing rapidly into enormous towers. A faint breeze sprang up, bringing with it the first of the monsoon raindrops. This was the moment everyone was waiting for. People ran out of their houses to take in the fresh breeze and the scent of those first few raindrops on the parched, dusty earth. Underground, in their cracks, the insects were moving. Termites and white ants, which had been sleeping through the hot season, emerged from their lairs.

And then, on the second or third night of the monsoon, came the great yearly flight of insects into the cool brief freedom of the night. Out of every crack, from under the roots of trees, huge winged ants emerged, at first fluttering about heavily, on the first and last flight of their lives. At night there was only one direction in which they could fly—towards the light; towards the electric bulbs and smoky kerosene lamps throughout Pipalnagar. The street lamp opposite the bus stop, beneath my room, attracted a massive quivering swarm of clumsy termites, which gave the impression of one thick, slowly revolving body.

This was the hour of the lizards. Now they had their reward for those days of patient waiting. Plying their sticky pink tongues, they devoured the insects as fast as they came. For hours, they crammed their stomachs, knowing that such a feast would not be theirs again for another year. How wasteful nature is, I thought. Through the whole hot season the insect world prepares for the flight out of the darkness into light and not one of them survives its freedom.

Suraj and I walked barefooted over the cool, wet pavements, across the railway lines and the riverbed, until we were not far from the crooked tree. Dotting the landscape were old abandoned brick kilns. When it rained heavily, the hollows made by the kilns filled up with water. Suraj and I found a small tank where we could bathe and swim. On a mound in the middle of the tank stood a ruined hut, formerly inhabited by a watchman at the kiln. We swam and then wrestled on the young green grass. Though I was heavier than Suraj and my chest as sound as a new drum, he had a lot of power in his long, wiry arms and legs, and he pinioned me about the waist with his bony knees.

And then suddenly, as I strained to press his back to the ground, I felt his body go tense. He stiffened, his thigh jerked against me and his legs began to twitch. I knew that a fit was coming on, but I was unable to get out of his grip. He held me more tightly as the fit took possession of him.

When I noticed his mouth working, I thrust the palm of my hand in, sideways to prevent him from biting his tongue. But so violent was the convulsion that his teeth bit into my flesh. I shouted with pain and tried to pull my hand away, but he was unconscious and his jaw was set. I closed my eyes and counted slowly up to seven and then I felt his muscles relax and I was able to take my hand away. It was bleeding a little but I bound it in a handkerchief before Suraj fully regained consciousness.

He didn't say much as we walked back to town. He looked depressed and weak, but I knew it wouldn't take long for him to recover his usual good spirits. He did not notice that I kept my hand out of sight and only after he had returned from classes that night did he notice the bandage and asked what happened.

X

'Do you want to make some money?' asked Pitamber, bursting into the room like a festive cracker.

'I do,' I said.

'What do we have to do for it?' asked Suraj, striking a cautious note.

'Oh nothing, carry a banner and walk in front of a procession.'

'Why?'

'Don't ask me. Some political stunt.'

'Which party?'

'I don't know. Who cares? All I know is that they are paying two rupees a day to anyone who'll carry a flag or banner.'

'We don't need two rupees that badly,' I said. 'And you can make more than that in a day with your rickshaw.'

'True, but they're paying me *five*. They're fixing a loudspeaker to my rickshaw, and one of the party's men will sit in it and make speeches as we go along. Come on, it will be fun.'

'No banners for us,' I said. 'But we may come along and watch.'

And we did watch, when, later that morning, the procession passed along our street. It was a ragged procession of about a hundred people, shouting slogans. Some of them were children, and some of them were men who did not know what it was all about, but all joined in the slogan-shouting.

We didn't know much about it, either. Because, though the man in Pitamber's rickshaw was loud and eloquent, his loudspeaker was defective, with the result that his words were punctuated with squeaks and an eerie whining sound. Pitamber looked up and saw us standing on the balcony and gave us a wave and a wide grin. We decided to follow the procession at a discreet distance. It was a protest march against something or other; we never did manage to find out the details. The destination was the municipal office, and by the time we got there the crowd had increased to two or three hundred people. Some rowdies had now joined in, and things began to get out of hand. The man in the rickshaw continued his speech; another man standing on a wall was making a speech; and someone from the municipal office was confronting the crowd and making a speech of his own.

A stone was thrown, then another. From a sprinkling of stones, it soon became a shower of stones; and then some police constables, who had been standing by watching the fun, were ordered into action. They ran at the crowd where it was thinnest, brandishing stout sticks.

We were caught in the stampede that followed. A stone—flung no doubt at a policeman—was badly aimed and struck me on the shoulder. Suraj pulled me down a side street. Looking back, we saw Pitamber's cycle rickshaw lying on its side in the middle of the road, but there was no sign of Pitamber.

Later, he turned up in my room, with a cut over his left eyebrow which was bleeding freely. Suraj washed the cut, and I poured iodine over it—Pitamber did not flinch—and covered it with sticking plaster. The cut was quite deep and should have had stitches, but Pitamber was superstitious about hospitals, saying he knew very few people to come out of them alive. He was of course thinking about the Pipalnagar hospital.

So he acquired a scar on his forehead. It went rather well with his demonic good looks.

XI

'Thank god for the monsoon,' said Suraj. 'We won't have any more demonstrations on the roads until the weather improves!'

And, until the rain stopped, Pipalnagar was fresh and clean and alive. The children ran naked out of their houses and romped through the streets. The gutters overflowed, and the road became a mountain stream, coursing merrily towards the bus stop.

At the bus stop there was confusion. Newly arrived passengers, surrounded on all sides by a sea of mud and rainwater, were met by scores of tongas and cycle rickshaws, each jostling the other trying to cater to the passengers. As a result, only half found conveyances, while the other half found themselves knee-deep in Pipalnagar mud.

Pipalnagar mud has a quality all its own—and it is not easily removed or forgotten. Only buffaloes love it because it is soft and squelchy. Two parts of it is thick sticky clay which seems to come alive at the slightest touch, clinging tenaciously to human flesh. Feet sink into it and have to be wrenched out. Fingers become webbed. Get it into your hair, and there is nothing you can do except go to Deep Chand and have your head shaved.

London has its fog, Paris its sewers, Pipalnagar its mud. Pitamber, of course, succeeded in getting as his passenger the most attractive girl to step off the bus, and showed her his skill and daring by taking her to her destination by the longest and roughest road.

The rain swirled over the trees and roofs of the town, and the parched earth soaked it up, giving out a fresh smell that came only once a year, the fragrance of quenched earth, that loveliest of all smells.

In my room I was battling against the elements, for the door would not close, and the rain swept into the room and soaked my cot. When finally I succeeded in closing the door, I discovered that the roof was leaking and the water was trickling down the walls, running through the dusty design I had made with my feet. I placed tins and mugs in strategic positions and, satisfied that everything was now under control, sat on the cot to watch the rooftops through my windows.

There was a loud banging on the door. It flew open, and there was Suraj, standing on the threshold, drenched. Coming in, he began to dry himself while I made desperate efforts to close the door again.

'Let's make some tea,' he said.

Glasses of hot, sweet milky tea on a rainy day…it was enough to make me feel fresh and full of optimism. We sat on the cot, enjoying the brew.

'One day, I'll write a book,' I said. 'Not just a thriller, but a real book, about real people. Perhaps about you and me and Pipalnagar. And then we'll be famous and our troubles will be over and new troubles will begin. I don't mind problems as long as they are new. While you're studying, I'll write my book. I'll start tonight. It is an auspicious time, the first night of the monsoon.

A tree must have fallen across the wires somewhere, because the lights would not come on. So I lit a small oil lamp, and while it spluttered in the steamy darkness, Suraj opened his book and, with one hand on the book, the other playing with his toe—this helped him to concentrate!—he began to study. I took the inkpot down from the shelf, and finding it empty, added a little rainwater to it from one of the mugs. I sat down beside Suraj and began to write, but the pen was no good and made blotches all over the paper. And, although I was full of writing just then, I didn't really know what I wanted to say.

So I went out and began pacing up and down the road. There I found Pitamber, a little drunk, very merry, and prancing about in the middle of the road.

'What are you dancing for?' I asked.

'I'm happy, so I'm dancing,' said Pitamber.

'And why are you happy?' I asked.

'Because I'm dancing,' he said.

The rain stopped and the neem trees gave out a strong, sweet smell.

XII

Flowers in Pipalnagar—did they exist? As a child I knew a garden in Lucknow where there were beds of phlox and petunias and another garden where only roses grew. In the fields around Pipalnagar was thorn apple—a yellow buttercup nestling among thorn leaves. But in the Pipalnagar bazaar, there were no flowers except one—marigold growing out of a crack on my balcony. I had removed the plaster from the base of the plant, and filled in a little earth which I watered every morning. The plant was healthy, and sometimes it produced a small orange marigold.

Sometimes Suraj plucked a flower and kept it in his tray, among the combs, buttons and scent bottles. Sometimes he gave the flower to passing child, once to a small boy who immediately tore it to shreds. Suraj was back on his rounds, as his exams were over.

Whenever he was tired of going from house to house, Suraj would sit beneath a shady banyan or pipal tree, put his tray aside, and take out his flute. The haunting notes travelled down the road in the afternoon stillness, drawing children to him. They would sit beside him and be very quiet when he played, because there was something melancholic and appealing about the tune. Suraj sometimes made flutes out of pieces of bamboo, but he never sold them. He would give them to the children he liked. He would sell almost anything, but not flutes.

Suraj sometimes played the flute at night, when he lay awake, unable to sleep; but even though I slept, I could hear the music in my dreams. Sometimes he took his flute with him to the crooked tree and played for the benefit of the birds. The parrots made harsh noises in response and flew away. Once, when Suraj was playing his flute to a small group of children, he had a fit. The flute fell from his hands. And he began to roll about in the dust on the roadside. The children became frightened and ran away, but they did not stay away for long. The next time they heard the flute, they came to listen as usual.

XIII

It was Lord Krishna's birthday, and the rain came down as heavily as it is said to have done on the day Krishna was born. Krishna is the best beloved of all the gods. Young mothers laugh or weep as they read or hear the pranks of his boyhood; young men pray to be as tall and as strong as Krishna was when he killed King Kamsa's elephant and wrestlers; young girls dream of a lover as daring as Krishna to carry them off in a war chariot; grown men envy the wisdom and statesmanship with which he managed the affairs of his kingdom.

The rain came so unexpectedly that it took everyone by surprise. In seconds, people were drenched, and within minutes, the streets were flooded. The temple tank overflowed, the railway lines disappeared, and the old wall near the bus stop shivered and silently fell—the sound of its collapse drowned in the downpour. A naked young man with a dancing bear cavorted in the middle of the vegetable market. Pitamber's rickshaw churned through the floodwater while he sang lustily as he worked.

Wading through knee-deep water down the road, I saw the roadside vendors salvaging whatever they could. Plastic toys, cabbages and utensils floated away and were seized by urchins. The water had risen to the level of the shop fronts and the floors were awash. Deep Chand and Ramu, with the help of a customer, were using buckets to bail the water out of their shop. The rain stopped as suddenly as it had begun and the sun came out. The water began to find an outlet, flooding other low-lying areas, and a paper boat came sailing between my legs.

Next morning, the morning on which the result of Suraj's examinations was due, I rose early—the first time I ever got up before Suraj—and went down to the news agency. A small crowd of students had gathered at the bus stop, joking with each other and hiding their nervousness with a show of indifference. There were not many passengers on the first bus, and there was a mad grab for newspapers as the bundle landed with a thud on the pavement. Within half-an-hour, the newsboy had sold all his copies. It was the best day of the year for him.

I went through the columns relating to Pipalnagar, but I couldn't find Suraj's roll number on the list of successful candidates. I had the number on a slip of paper, and I looked at it again to make sure I had compared it correctly with the others; then I went through the newspaper once more. When I returned to the room, Suraj was sitting on the doorstep. I didn't have to tell him he had failed—he knew by the look on my face. I sat down beside him, and we said nothing for some time.

'Never mind,' Suraj said eventually. 'I will pass next year.'

I realized I was more depressed than he was and that he was trying to console me.

'If only you'd had more time,' I said.

'I have plenty of time now. Another year. And you will have time to finish your book, and then we can go away together. Another year of Pipalnagar won't be so bad. As long as I have your friendship almost everything can be tolerated.'

He stood up, the tray hanging from his shoulders. 'What would you like to buy?'

XIV

Another year of Pipalnagar! But it was not to be. A short time later, I received a letter from the editor of a newspaper, calling me to Delhi for an interview. My friends insisted that I should go. Such an opportunity would not come again.

But I needed a shirt. The few I possessed were either frayed at the collar or torn at the shoulders. I hadn't been able to afford a new shirt for over a year, and I couldn't afford one now. Struggling writers weren't expected to dress well, but I felt in order to get the job I would need both a haircut and a clean shirt.

Where was I to go to get a shirt? Suraj generally wore an old red-striped T-shirt; he washed it every second evening, and by morning it was dry and ready to wear again; but it was tight even on him. He did not have another. Besides, I needed something white, something respectable!

I went to Deep Chand who had a collection of shirts. He was only too glad to lend me one. But they were all brightly coloured—pinks, purples and magentas… No editor was going to be impressed by a young writer in a pink shirt. They looked fine on Deep Chand, but he had no need to look respectable.

Finally, Pitamber came to my rescue. He didn't bother with shirts himself, except in winter, but he was able to borrow a clean white shirt from a guard at the jail, who'd got it from the relative of a convict in exchange for certain favours.

'This shirt will make you look respectable,' said Pitamber. 'To be respectable—what an adventure!'

XV

Freedom. The moment the bus was out of Pipalnagar, and the

fields opened out on all sides, I knew that I was free, that I had always been free. Only my own weakness, hesitation, and the habits that had grown around me had held me back. All I had to do was sit in a bus and go somewhere.

I sat near the open window of the bus and let the cool breeze from the fields play against my face. Herons and snipe waded among the lotus roots in flat green ponds. Blue jays swooped around telegraph poles. Children jumped naked into the canals that wound through the fields. Because I was happy, it seemed to me that everyone else was happy—the driver, the conductor, the passengers, the farmers in the fields and those driving bullock-carts. When two women behind me started quarrelling over their seats. I helped to placate them. Then I took a small girl on my knee and pointed out camels, buffaloes, vultures and pariah dogs.

Six hours later, the bus crossed the bridge over the swollen Jamuna river, passed under the walls of the great Red Fort built by a Mughal emperor, and entered the old city of Delhi. I found it strange to be in a city again, after several years in Pipalnagar. It was a little frightening too. I felt like a stranger. No one was interested in me.

In Pipalnagar, people wanted to know each other, or at least to know about one another. In Delhi, no one cared who you were or where you came from, like big cities almost everywhere. It was prosperous but without a heart.

After a day and a night of loneliness, I found myself wishing that Suraj had accompanied me; wishing that I was back in Pipalnagar. But when the job was offered to me—at a starting salary of three hundred rupees per month, a princely sum compared to what I had been making on my own—I did not have the courage to refuse it. After accepting the job—which was to commence in a week's time—I spent the day wandering through the bazaars, down the wide shady roads of the capital, resting under the jamun trees, and thinking all the time what I would do in the months to come.

I slept at the railway waiting room and all night long I heard the shunting and whistling of engines which conjured up visions of places with sweet names like Kumbakonam, Krishnagiri, Polonnarurawa. I dreamt of palm-fringed beaches and inland lagoons; of the echoing chambers of deserted cities, red sandstone and white marble; of temples in the sun; and elephants crossing wide slow-moving rivers...

XVI

Pitamber was on the platform when the train steamed into the Pipalnagar station in the early hours of a damp September morning. I waved to him from the carriage window, and shouted that everything had gone well.

But everything was not well here. When I got off the train, Pitamber told me that Suraj had been ill—that he'd had a fit on a lonely stretch of road the previous afternoon and had lain in the sun for over an hour. Pitamber had found him, suffering from heatstroke, and brought him home. When I saw him, he was sitting up on the string bed drinking hot tea. He looked pale and weak, but his smile was reassuring.

'Don't worry,' he said. 'I will be all right.'

'He was bad last night,' said Pitamber. 'He had a fever and kept talking, as in a dream. But what he says is true—he is better this morning.'

'Thanks to Pitamber,' said Suraj. 'It is good to have friends.'

'Come with me to Delhi, Suraj,' I said. 'I have got a job now. You can live with me and attend a school regularly.'

'It is good for friends to help each other,' said Suraj, 'but only after I have passed my exam will I join you in Delhi. I made myself this promise. Poor Pipalnagar—nobody wants to stay here. Will you be sorry to leave?'

'Yes, I will be sorry. A part of me will still be here.'

XVII

Deep Chand was happy to know that I was leaving. 'I'll follow you soon,' he said. 'There is money to be made in Delhi, cutting hair. Girls are keeping it short these days.'

'But men are growing it long.'

'True. So I shall open a barbershop for ladies and a beauty salon for men! Ramu can attend to the ladies.'

Ramu winked at me in the mirror. He was still at the stage of teasing girls on their way to school or college.

The snip of Deep Chand's scissors made me sleepy, as I sat in his chair. His fingers beat a rhythmic tattoo on my scalp. It was my last haircut in Pipalnagar, and Deep Chand did not charge me for it. I promised to write as soon as I had settled down in Delhi.

The next day when Suraj was stronger, I said, 'Come, let us go for a walk and visit our crooked tree. Where is your flute, Suraj?'

'I don't know. Let us look for it.'

We searched the room and our belongings for the flute but could not find it.

'It must have been left on the roadside,' said Suraj. 'Never mind. I will make another.'

I could picture the flute lying in the dust on the roadside and somehow this made me sad. But Suraj was full of high spirits as we walked across the railway lines and through the fields.

'The rains are over,' he said, kicking off his chappals and lying down on the grass. 'You can smell the autumn in the air. Somehow, it makes me feel light-hearted. Yesterday I was sad, and tomorrow I might be sad again, but today I know that I am happy. I want to live on and on. One lifetime cannot satisfy my heart.'

'A day in a lifetime,' I said. 'I'll remember this day—the way the sun touches us, the way the grass bends, the smell of this leaf as I crush it...'

XVIII

At six every morning the first bus arrives, and the passengers alight, looking sleepy and dishevelled, and rather discouraged by their first sight of Pipalnagar. When they have gone their various ways, the bus is driven into the shed. Cows congregate at the dustbin and the pavement dwellers come to life, stretching their tired limbs on the hard stone steps. I carry the bucket up the steps to my room, and bathe for the last time on the open balcony. In the villages, the buffaloes are wallowing in green ponds while naked urchins sit astride them, scrubbing their backs, and a crow or water bird perches on their glistening necks. The parrots are busy in the crooked tree, and a slim green snake basks in the sun on our island near the brick-kiln. In the hills, the mists have lifted and the distant mountains are fringed with snow.

It is autumn, and the rains are over. The earth meets the sky in one broad bold sweep.

A land of thrusting hills. Terraced hills, wood-covered and windswept. Mountains where the gods speak gently to the lonely. Hills of green grass and grey rock, misty at dawn, hazy at noon, molten at sunset, where fierce fresh torrents rush to the valleys below. A quiet land of fields and ponds, shaded by ancient trees and ringed with palms, where sacred rivers are touched by temples, where temples are touched by southern seas.

This is the land I should write about. Pipalnagar should be forgotten. I should turn aside from it to sing instead of the splendours of exotic places.

But only yesterdays are truly splendid... And there are other singers, sweeter than I, to sing of tomorrow. I can only write of today, of Pipalnagar, where I have lived and loved.

A FACE IN THE DARK

Mr Oliver, an Anglo-Indian teacher, was returning to his school late one night, on the outskirts of the hill station of Simla. From before Kipling's time, the school had been run on English public school lines and the boys, most of them from wealthy Indian families, wore blazers, caps and ties. *Life* magazine, in a feature on India, had once called it the 'Eton of the East'. Mr Oliver had been teaching in the school for several years.

The Simla bazaar, with its cinemas and restaurants, was about three miles from the school and Mr Oliver, a bachelor, usually strolled into the town in the evening, returning after dark, when he would take a shortcut through the pine forest.

When there was a strong wind, the pine trees made sad, eerie sounds that kept most people to the main road. But Mr Oliver was not a nervous or imaginative man. He carried a torch and its gleam—the batteries were running down—moved fitfully down the narrow forest path. When its flickering light fell on the figure of a boy who was sitting alone on a rock, Mr Oliver stopped. Boys were not supposed to be out after dark.

'What are you doing out here, boy?' asked Mr Oliver sharply, moving closer so that he could recognize the miscreant. But even as he approached the boy, Mr Oliver sensed that something was wrong. The boy appeared to be crying. His head hung down, he held his face in his hands, and his body shook convulsively. It was a strange, soundless weeping and Mr Oliver felt distinctly uneasy.

'Well, what's the matter?' he asked, his anger giving way to concern. 'What are you crying for?' The boy would not answer or look up. His body continued to be racked with silent sobbing.

'Come on, boy, you shouldn't be out here at this hour. Tell me the trouble. Look up!' The boy looked up. He took his hands from his face and looked up at his teacher. The light from Mr Oliver's torch fell on the boy's face—if you could call it a face.

It had no eyes, ears, nose or mouth. It was just a round smooth head—with a school cap on top of it! And that's where the story should end. But for Mr Oliver it did not end here.

The torch fell from his trembling hand. He turned and scrambled down the path, running blindly through the trees and calling for help. He was still running blindly towards the school buildings when he saw a lantern swinging in the middle of the path. Mr Oliver stumbled up to the watchman, gasping for breath. 'What is it, sahib?' asked the watchman. 'Has there been an accident? Why are you running?'

'I saw something—something horrible—a boy weeping in the forest—and he had no face!'

'No face, sahib?'

'No eyes, nose, mouth—nothing!'

'Do you mean it was like this, sahib?' asked the watchman and raised the lamp to his own face. The watchman had no eyes, no ears, no features at all—not even an eyebrow! And that's when the wind blew the lamp out.

THE SKULL

I am not normally bothered by skeletons and old bones—they are, after all, just the chalky remains of the long dead—so when my nephew Anil came back from medical college with a well-preserved skull, it was no cause for alarm. He was a second year student, at times a bit of a prankster.

'I hope you didn't take it without permission,' I said, taking the skull in my hands and admiring its symmetry but without philosophizing upon it like Hamlet.

'Oh, the college is full of them,' said Anil. 'I just borrowed it for the vacation.' He placed it on the mantelpiece, among some of the awards and mementos (cheap brassware mostly) that had accumulated over the years, and I must say it livened up the shelf a little.

Anil had placed the skull at one end of the mantelpiece, and there it stood until we'd had our dinner. He settled down with a book, while I poured myself a small glass of cognac before settling into an easy chair with a notebook on my knee. It was midsummer, and the window was open, so that we could hear the crickets singing in the oak trees. My cottage was on the outskirts of Mussoorie, surrounded by Himalayan oak and maple.

I had been making some notes for an article on wild flowers. When I had finished my notes and my cognac, I looked up and noticed that the skull now stood in the centre of the mantelpiece.

'Did you move the skull?' I asked.

'No,' said Anil, looking up. 'I placed it at the end of the shelf.'

'Well, it's now in the middle. How did it get there?'

'You must have moved it yourself, without noticing. That was a stiff cognac you drank, Uncle.'

I let it pass, it did not seem important.

※

People often dropped in to see me. Schoolteachers, visitors to the hill station, students, other writers, neighbours. During that week I had a number of visitors, and of course everyone noticed the skull on the mantelpiece. Some were intrigued, and wanted to know whose skull it was. One or two lady teachers were frightened by it. A fellow writer thought it was in bad taste, displaying human remains in my sitting room. One visitor offered to buy it.

I would gladly have sold the wretched thing, but it belonged to Anil and he intended to take it back to Meerut. But when the time came to leave he forgot about the skull, his mind no doubt taken up with other matters—such as the daily phone calls he received from a girl student in Delhi. After seeing him off at the bus stop, I came home to find that the skull was still occupying pride of place on the mantelpiece.

I ignored it for a few days, and the skull didn't seem to mind that. It was receiving plenty of attention from visitors during the day.

But it was beginning to get on my nerves. Every evening, when I sat down to enjoy a whisky or a cognac, I would feel its empty eye sockets staring at me. And on one occasion, when I tried to change its position, my hand got caught in its jawbone and it was with some difficulty that I withdrew it.

Getting fed up of its presence, I decided to lock the thing away where it wouldn't be seen.

There was a wall cupboard in the room, where I kept my manuscripts, notebooks, and writing materials, and there was plenty of space there for the skull. So I shifted it to the cupboard, and made sure the doors were locked.

That evening I enjoyed my drink without being watched

by that remnant of a human head. The crickets were singing, a nightjar was calling, and a zephyr of a wind moved softly through the trees. I finished my article and went to bed in a happy frame of mind.

In the middle of the night I woke to a loud rattling sound. At first I thought it was a loose door latch or a wobbly drainpipe, then realized the noise was coming from the wall cupboard. A rat, perhaps? But no. As soon as I opened the cupboard door, out popped the skull, landing near my feet and bouncing away right across the drawing room.

For the sake of peace and quiet, I returned it to the mantelpiece. If a skull could smile, it would probably have done so. I went back to my bed and slept like a baby. It takes more than a dancing skull to keep me from enjoying a good night's sleep.

The next morning I got to work making up a parcel. Normally, I hate making parcels, they usually fall apart. But for once I took pleasure in making a parcel. I wrapped the skull in a plastic bag, then placed it in a strong cardboard box, wrapped this in brown parcel paper, used a liberal amount of Sellotape, and addressed the package to Dr Anil at his medical college. Then I walked into town and handed it over to the registration clerk at the post office.

Rubbing my hands with satisfaction, I treated myself to fish and chips and an ice cream before setting out on the walk down the hill to my cottage.

I was about halfway down the steep path that leads to one of our famous schools when I heard something rattling down the slope behind me. At first I thought it was an empty tin, but then I recognized my boon companion, that wretched skull, embellished with bits of wrapping paper and Sellotape, bouncing down the hill towards me. How did the skull get out of that parcel? I shall never know. Perhaps a nosy postal clerk had opened it to check the contents. I hope he got the fright of his life. I broke into a run, making a dash for the cottage door. But it was there before me, grinning up at me from a pot full of flowering petunias.

So back it went to its favourite place on the mantelpiece. And there it remained for several weeks.

🌺

The school's playing field was situated just above the path to the cottage, and during the football season I could hear the boys kicking a football around.

One day a football escaped from the field and came bouncing down the hillside, landing on a flower bed. The match was over and no one bothered to come down to retrieve the ball. But it gave me an idea. I removed the bladder, stuffed the skull into the leather interior, and tied it up firmly. Then I had the football delivered to the school's games master, with my compliments.

Nothing happened for a couple of days. There was no shortage of footballs. Then in the middle of the game against St George's College, a ball went out of the grounds and a spare one was required.

The replacement did not bounce quite as well as the previous one, and it was inclined to spin around a lot and take off in directions opposite to those intended. Also, it squeaked whenever it received a kick, and sometimes those squeaks sounded a bit like screams of protest. The goalkeepers at either end found the ball difficult to hold, it did its best to elude their grasp. And more goals were scored by accident rather than design. Finally, this eccentric ball was kicked out of play and was replaced by another.

What happens to old footballs? I expect they finally fall apart and end up in a dustbin.

In this case, the football found a new owner, for the sports master was a kind man who gave away old bats, balls and other worn-out stuff to the poor children of the locality. A boy from a village near Rajpur was the recipient of the battered football, and he and his friends carried it away with a cheer, kicking it all the way down the steep path, making so much noise that they did not hear the groans of protest that issued from the battered old football.

Well, weeks passed, months passed, without the skull making a reappearance. But then something strange began to happen. I found myself missing that troublesome skull!

It had, after all, been company of a sort for a lonely writer living on his own on the edge of the forest. And when you have lived with someone for a long time, then, no matter how much you may quarrel or get on each other's nerves, a bond is formed, and the strength of that bond can only be known when it is broken.

The skull had been sharing my life for over a year, and now that it was gone, seemingly forever, my life seemed rather empty.

So I began searching for the skull. I enquired amongst the children down in Rajpur, but they had long since lost the football. I made a round of all the junk shops in Dehradun, without any luck. There were lots of old footballs lying around, but not the one I wanted. And, no, they didn't buy or sell human skulls.

Young Anil, the doctor, paid me a brief visit and found me looking depressed.

'What's the trouble?' he asked. 'You look as though you've just lost a friend.'

'I have, indeed,' I said. 'I miss that skull you gave me. It was company of a sort.'

'Well, I'll get you another. No shortage of skulls in my college.'

'No, I don't want another. I want the same skull. It had a personality of its own.'

Anil looked at me as though he thought I was going off my rocker. And perhaps I was.

And then one day, as I was walking down a busy street in neighbouring Saharanpur, I noticed a fortune teller plying his trade on the pavement. I don't believe in fortune telling, but everyone has to make a living, and telling fortunes seems to me a harmless way of doing it. And then I noticed that he had a skull beside him, and that he would consult it before handing his customer a slip of paper with words of advice or encouragement written on it. It looked a bit like my skull, but I couldn't be sure. All the kicking and manhandling it had received had possibly altered its appearance.

But, anyway, I gave the fortune teller some money and asked him for a prediction. He chanted something, then extracted a slip of paper from beneath the skull and handed it to me with a flourish.

I read the words printed neatly on the paper.

'Ullu ka patha', went the message, followed by 'Gadhe ka baccha!'

It was definitely my skull! Only an old friend could abuse me like that.

So I pleaded and haggled with the fortune teller, paid him a hundred rupees for the skull, and carried it home in triumph.

And there it is today, decorating my mantelpiece, a little the worse for wear, and with a silly grin on its skeletal face. To improve its looks I have placed an old cricket cap on its head.

Sometimes we don't value our friends until we lose them.

MY FATHER'S TREES IN DEHRA

Our trees still grow in Dehra. This is one part of the world where trees are a match for man. An old pipal may be cut down to make way for a new building; two pipal trees will sprout from the walls of the building. In Dehra the air is moist, the soil hospitable to seeds and probing roots. The valley of Dehradun lies between the first range of the Himalayas and the smaller but older Shivalik range. Dehra is an old town, but it was not in the reign of Rajput princes or Mughal kings that it really grew and flourished; it acquired a certain size and importance with the coming of the British and Anglo-Indian settlers. The English have an affinity with trees, and in the rolling hills of Dehra they discovered a retreat which, in spite of snakes and mosquitoes, reminded them, just a little bit, of England's green and pleasant land.

The mountains to the north are austere and inhospitable; the plains to the south are flat, dry and dusty. But Dehra is green. I look out of the train window at daybreak to see the sal and shisham trees sweep by majestically, while trailing vines and great clumps of bamboo give the forest a darkness and density which add to its mystery. There are still a few tigers in these forests, only a few, and perhaps they will survive, to stalk the spotted deer and drink at forest pools.

I grew up in Dehra. My grandfather built a bungalow on the outskirts of the town at the turn of the century. The house was sold a few years after Independence. No one knows me now in Dehra, for it is over twenty years since I left the place, and my boyhood friends are scattered and lost. And although the India of *Kim* is no more, and the Grand Trunk Road is now a procession of trucks instead of a slow-moving caravan of horses and camels, India is still a country in which people are easily lost and quickly forgotten.

From the station I can take either a taxi or a snappy little scooter rickshaw (Dehra had neither before 1950), but because I am on an unashamedly sentimental pilgrimage, I take a tonga, drawn by a lean, listless pony, and driven by a tubercular old Muslim man in a shabby green waistcoat. Only two or three tongas stand outside the station. There were always twenty or thirty here in the 1940s when I came home from boarding school to be met at the station by my grandfather; but the days of the tonga are nearly over, and in many ways this is a good thing, because most tonga ponies are overworked and underfed. Its wheels squeaking from lack of oil and its seat slipping out from under me, the tonga drags me through the bazaars of Dehra. A couple of miles of this slow, funereal pace makes me impatient to use my own legs, and I dismiss the tonga when we get to the small Dilaram bazaar.

It is a good place from which to start walking.

The Dilaram bazaar has not changed very much. The shops are run by a new generation of bakers, barbers and banias, but professions have not changed. The cobblers belong to the lower castes, the bakers are Muslims, the tailors are Sikhs. Boys still fly kites from the flat rooftops, and women wash clothes on the canal steps. The canal comes down from Rajpur and goes underground here, to emerge about a mile away.

I have to walk only a furlong to reach my grandfather's house. The road is lined with eucalyptus, jacaranda and laburnum trees. In the compounds there are small groves of mangoes, litchis and papayas. The poinsettia thrusts its scarlet leaves over garden walls. Every veranda has its bougainvillea creeper, every garden its bed of marigolds. Potted palms, those symbols of Victorian snobbery, are popular with Indian housewives. There are a few houses, but most of the bungalows were built by 'old India hands' on their retirement from the army, the police or the railways. Most of the present owners are Indian businessmen or government officials.

I am standing outside my grandfather's house. The wall has been raised, and the wicket gate has disappeared. I cannot get a clear view of the house and garden. The nameplate identifies the owner as Major General Saigal; the house has had more than one owner since my grandparents sold it in 1949.

On the other side of the road there is an orchard of litchi trees. This is not the season for fruit, and there is no one looking after the garden. By taking a little path that goes through the orchard, I reach higher ground and gain a better view of our old house.

Grandfather built the house with granite rocks taken from the foothills. It shows no sign of age. The lawn has disappeared, but the big jackfruit tree, giving shade to the side veranda, is still there. On this tree I spent my afternoons, absorbed in my Magnets, Champions and Hotspurs, while sticky mango juice trickled down my chin. (One could not eat the jackfruit unless it was cooked into a vegetable curry.) There was a hole in the bole of the tree in which I kept my pocket knife, top, catapult and any badges or buttons that could be saved from my father's RAF tunics when he came home on leave. There was also an Iron Cross, a relic of World War I, given to me by my grandfather. I have managed to keep the Iron Cross, but what did I do with my top and catapult? Memory fails me. Possibly they are still in the hole in the jackfruit tree; I must have forgotten to collect them when we went away after my father's death. I am seized by a whimsical urge to walk in at the gate, climb into the branches of the jackfruit tree and recover my lost possessions. What would the present owner, the major general (retired), have to say if I politely asked permission to look for a catapult left behind more than twenty years ago?

An old man is coming down the path through the litchi trees. He is not a major general but a poor street vendor. He carries a small tin trunk on his head, and walks very slowly. When he sees me, he stops and asks me if I will buy something. I can think of nothing I need, but the old man looks so tired, so very old, that I am afraid he will collapse if he moves any further along the path without resting. So I ask him to show me his wares. He cannot get the box off his head by himself, but together we manage to set it down in the shade, and the old man insists on spreading its contents on the grass: bangles, combs, shoelaces, safety pins, cheap stationery, buttons, pomades, elastic and scores of other household necessities.

When I refuse buttons because there is no one to sew them on for me, he plies me with safety pins. I say no, but as he moves from one article to another, his querulous, persuasive voice slowly wears down my resistance, and I end up buying envelopes, a letter pad (pink roses on bright blue paper), a one-rupee fountain pen guaranteed to leak, and several yards of elastic. I have no idea what I will do with the elastic, but the old man convinces me that I cannot live without it.

Exhausted by the effort of selling me a lot of things I obviously do not want, he closes his eyes and leans back against the trunk of a litchi tree. For a moment I feel rather nervous. Is he going to die sitting here beside me? He sinks to his haunches and puts his chin on his hands. He only wants to talk.

'I am very tired, huzoor,' he says. 'Please do not mind if I sit here for a while.'

'Rest for as long as you like,' I say. 'That's a heavy load you've been carrying.'

He comes to life at the chance of a conversation and says, 'When I was a young man, it was nothing. I could carry my box up from Rajpur to Mussoorie by the bridle path—seven steep miles! But now I find it difficult to cover the distance from the station to Dilaram bazaar.'

'Naturally. You are quite old.'

'I am seventy, sahib.'

'You look very fit for your age,' I say this to please him; he looks frail and brittle. 'Isn't there someone to help you?' I ask.

'I had a servant boy last month, but he stole my earnings and ran off to Delhi. I wish my son was alive—he would not have permitted me to work like a mule for a living—but he was killed in the riots in 1947.'

'Have you no other relatives?'

'I have outlived them all. That is the curse of a healthy life. Your friends, your loved ones, all go before you, and at the end you are left alone. But I must go too, before long. The road to the bazaar seems to grow longer every day. The stones are harder. The sun is hotter in the summer, and the wind much colder in the winter. Even some of the trees that were there in my youth have grown old and have died. I have outlived the trees.'

He has outlived the trees. He is like an old tree himself, gnarled and twisted. I have the feeling that if he falls asleep in the orchard, he will strike root here, sending out crooked branches. I can imagine a small bent tree wearing a black waistcoat, a living scarecrow.

He closes his eyes again, but goes on talking.

'The English memsahibs would buy great quantities of elastic. Today it is ribbons and bangles for the girls, and combs for the boys. But I do not make much money. Because I cannot walk very far. How many houses do I reach in a day? Ten, fifteen. But twenty years ago I could visit more than fifty houses. That makes a difference.'

'Have you always been here?'

'Most of my life, huzoor. I was here before they built the motor road to Mussoorie. I was here when the sahibs had their own carriages and ponies and the memsahibs their own rickshaws. I was here before there were any cinemas. I was here when the Prince of Wales came to Dehradun... Oh, I have been here a long time, huzoor. I was here when that house was built,' he says, pointing with his chin towards my grandfather's house. 'Fifty, sixty years ago it must have been. I cannot remember exactly. What is ten years when you have lived seventy? But it was a tall, red-bearded sahib who built that house. He kept many creatures as pets. A kachwa (turtle) was one of them. And there was a python which crawled into my box one day and gave me a terrible fright. The sahib used to keep it hanging from his shoulders, like a garland. His wife, the burra mem, always bought a lot from me—lots of elastic. And there were sons, one a teacher, another in the air force, and there were always children in the house. Beautiful children. But they went away many years ago. Everyone has gone away.'

I do not tell him that I am one of the 'beautiful children', I doubt if he will believe me. His memories are of another age, another place, and for him there are no strong bridges into the present.

'But others have come,' I say.

'True, and that is as it should be. That is not my complaint. My complaint—should god be listening—is that I have been left behind.'

He gets slowly to his feet and stands over his shabby tin box, gazing down at it with a mixture of disdain and affection. I help him to lift and balance it on the flattened cloth on his head. He does not have the energy to turn and make a salutation of any kind, but, setting his sights on the distant hills, he walks down the path with steps that are shaky and slow but still wonderfully straight.

I wonder how much longer he will live. Perhaps a year or two, perhaps a week, perhaps an hour. It will be an end of living, but it will not be death. He is too old for death; he can only sleep; he can only fall gently, like an old, crumpled brown leaf.

I leave the orchard. The bend in the road hides my grandfather's house. I reach the canal again. It emerges from under a small culvert, where maidenhair ferns grow in the shade.

My Father's Trees in Dehra

The water, coming from a stream in the foothills, rushes along with a familiar sound; it does not lose its momentum until the canal has left the gently sloping streets of the town.

There are new buildings on this road, but the small police station is housed in the same old lime-washed bungalow. A couple of off-duty policemen, partly uniformed but with their pyjamas on, stroll hand in hand on the grass verge. Holding hands (with persons of the same sex, of course) is common practice in northern India, and denotes no special relationship.

I cannot forget this little police station. Nothing very exciting ever happened in its vicinity until, in 1947, communal riots broke out in Dehra. Then, bodies were regularly fished out of the canal and dumped on a growing pile in the station compound. I was only a boy, but when I looked over the wall at that pile of corpses, there was no one who paid any attention to me. They were too busy to send me away. At the same time they knew that I was perfectly safe. While Hindus and Muslims were at each other's throats, a white boy could walk the streets in safety. No one was any longer interested in the Europeans.

The people of Dehra are not violent by nature, and the town has no history of communal discord. But when refugees from partitioned Punjab poured into Dehra in the thousands, the atmosphere became charged with tension. These refugees, many of them Sikhs, had lost their homes and livelihoods; many had seen their loved ones butchered. They were in a fierce and vengeful frame of mind. The calm, sleepy atmosphere of Dehra was shattered during two months of looting and murder. Those Muslims who could get away, fled. The poorer members of the community remained in a refugee camp until the holocaust was over, then they returned to their former occupations, frightened and deeply mistrustful. The old box-man was one of them.

I cross the canal and take the road that will lead me to the riverbed. This was one of my father's favourite walks. He, too, was a walking man. Often, when he was home on leave, he would say, 'Ruskin, let's go for a walk,' and we would slip off together and walk down to the riverbed or into the sugarcane fields or across the railway lines and into the jungle.

On one of these walks (this was before Independence), I remember him saying, 'After the war is over, we'll be going to England. Would you like that?'

'I don't know,' I said. 'Can't we stay in India?'

'It won't be ours anymore.'

'Has it always been ours?' I asked.

'For a long time,' he said, 'over two hundred years. But we have to give it back now.'

'Give it back to whom?' I asked. I was only nine.

'To the Indians,' said my father.

The only Indians I had known till then were my ayah and the cook and the gardener and their children, and I could not imagine them wanting to be rid of us. The only other Indian who came to the house was Dr Ghose, and it was frequently said of him that he was more English than the English. I could understand my father better when he said, 'After the war, there'll be a job for me in England. There'll be nothing for me here.'

The war had at first been a distant event, but somehow it kept coming closer. My aunt, who lived in London with her two children, was killed with them during an air raid, then my father's younger brother died of dysentery on the long walk out from Burma. Both these tragic events depressed my father. Never in good health (he had been prone to attacks of malaria), he looked more worn and wasted every time he came home. His personal life was far from being happy, as he and my mother had separated, she to marry again. I think he looked forward a great deal to the days he spent with me; far more than I could have realized at the time. I was someone to come back to, someone for whom things could be planned, someone who could learn from him.

Dehra suited him. He was always happy when he was among

trees, and this happiness communicated itself to me. I felt like drawing close to him. I remember sitting beside him on the veranda steps when I noticed the tendril of a creeping vine that was trailing near my feet. As we sat there, doing nothing in particular—in the best gardens, time has no meaning—I found that the tendril was moving almost imperceptibly away from me and towards my father. Twenty minutes later it had crossed the veranda steps and was touching his feet. This, in India, is the sweetest of salutations.

There is probably a scientific explanation for the plant's behaviour—something to do with the light and warmth on the veranda steps—but I like to think that its movements were motivated simply by affection for my father. Sometimes, when I sat alone beneath a tree, I felt a little lonely or lost. As soon as my father rejoined me, the atmosphere lightened, the tree itself became more friendly.

Most of the fruit trees round the house were planted by Father, but he was not content with planting trees in the garden. On rainy days we would walk beyond the riverbed, armed with cutting and saplings and then we would amble through the jungle, planting flowering shrubs between the sal and shisham trees.

'But no one ever comes here,' I protested the first time. 'Who is going to see them?'

'Some day,' he said, 'someone may come this way... If people keep cutting trees instead of planting them, there'll soon be no forests left at all, and the world will be just one vast desert.'

The prospect of a world without trees became a sort of nightmare for me (and one reason why I shall never want to live on a treeless moon), and I assisted my father in his tree planting with great enthusiasm.

'One day the trees will move again,' he said. 'They've been standing still for thousands of years. There was a time when they could walk about like people, but someone cast a spell on them and rooted them to one place. But they're always trying to move—see how they reach out with their arms!'

We found an island, a small rocky island in the middle of a dry riverbed. It was one of those riverbeds, so common in the foothills, which are completely dry in the summer but flooded during the monsoon rains. The rains had just begun, and the stream could still be crossed on foot, when we set out with a number of tamarind, laburnum and coral tree saplings and cuttings. We spent the day planting them on the island, then ate our lunch there, in the shelter of a wild plum.

My father went away soon after that tree planting. Three months later, in Calcutta, he died.

I was sent to boarding school. My grandparents sold the house and left Dehra. After school, I went to England. Years passed, my grandparents died, and when I returned to India I was the only member of the family in the country.

And now I am in Dehra again, on the road to the riverbed.

The houses with their trim gardens are soon behind me, and I am walking through fields of flowering mustard, which make a carpet of yellow blossoms stretching away towards the jungle and the foothills.

The riverbed is dry at this time of the year. A herd of skinny cattle graze on the short brown grass at the edge of the jungle. The sal trees have been thinned out. Could our trees have survived? Will our island be there, or has some flash flood during a heavy monsoon washed it away completely?

As I look across the dry watercourse, my eye is caught by the spectacular red plumes of the coral blossom. In contrast with the dry, rocky riverbed, the little island is a green oasis. I walk across to the trees and notice that a number of parrots have come to live in them. A koel challenges me with a rising 'who-are-you, who-are-you…'

But the trees seem to know me. They whisper among themselves and beckon me nearer. And, looking around, I find that other trees and wild plants and grasses have sprung up under the protection of the trees we planted.

They have multiplied. They are moving. In this small forgotten corner of the world, my father's dreams are coming true and the trees are moving again.

A CASE FOR INSPECTOR LAL

I met Inspector Keemat Lal about two years ago, while I was living in the hot, dusty town of Shahpur in the plains of northern India.

Keemat Lal had charge of the local police station. He was a heavily built man, slow and rather ponderous, and inclined to be lazy; but, like most lazy people, he was intelligent. He was also a failure. He had remained an inspector for a number of years, and had given up all hope of further promotion. His luck was against him, he said. He should never have been a policeman. He had been born under the sign of Capricorn and should really have gone into the restaurant business, but now it was too late to do anything about it.

The inspector and I had little in common. He was nearing forty, and I was twenty-five. But both of us spoke English, and in Shahpur there were very few people who did. In addition, we were both fond of beer. There were no places of entertainment in Shahpur. The searing heat, the dust that came whirling up from the east, the mosquitoes (almost as numerous as the flies), and the general monotony gave one a thirst for something more substantial than stale lemonade.

My house was on the outskirts of the town, where we were not often disturbed. On two or three evenings in the week, just as the sun was going down and making it possible for one to emerge from the khas-cooled confines of a dark, high-ceilinged bedroom, Inspector Keemat Lal would appear on the veranda steps, mopping the sweat from his face with a small towel, which he used instead of a handkerchief. My only servant, excited at the prospect of serving an inspector of police, would hurry out with glasses, a bucket of ice and several bottles of the best Indian beer.

One evening, after we had overtaken our fourth bottle, I said, 'You must have had some interesting cases in your career, Inspector.'

'Most of them were rather dull,' he said. 'At least the successful ones were. The sensational cases usually went unsolved—otherwise I might have been a superintendent by now. I suppose you are talking of murder cases. Do you remember the shooting of the minister of the interior? I was on that one, but it was a political murder and we never solved it.'

'Tell me about a case you solved,' I said. 'An interesting one.' When I saw him looking uncomfortable, I added, 'You don't have to worry, Inspector. I'm a very discreet person, in spite of all the beer I consume.'

'But how can you be discreet? You are a writer.'

I protested, 'Writers are usually very discreet. They always change the names of people and places.'

He gave me one of his rare smiles, 'And how would you describe me, if you were to put me into a story?'

'Oh, I'd leave you as you are. No one would believe in you, anyway.'

He laughed indulgently and poured out more beer. 'I suppose I can change names, too... I will tell you of a very interesting case. The victim was an unusual person, and so was the killer. But you must promise not to write this story.'

'I promise,' I lied.

'Do you know Panauli?'

'In the hills? Yes, I have been there once or twice.'

'Good, then you will follow me without my having to be too descriptive. This happened about three years ago, shortly after I had been stationed at Panauli. Nothing ever happened there. There were a few cases of theft and cheating, and an occasional fight during the summer. A murder took place about once every ten years. It was therefore quite an event when the Rani of —— was found dead in her sitting room, her head split open with an axe. I knew that I would have to solve the case if I wanted to stay in Panauli.

'The trouble was, anyone could have killed the rani, and there were some who made no secret of their satisfaction that she was dead. She had been an unpopular woman. Her husband was dead, her children were scattered, and her money—for she had never been a very wealthy rani—had been dwindling away. She lived alone in an old house on the outskirts of the town, ruling the locality with the stern authority of a matriarch. She had a servant, and he was the man who found the body and came to the police, dithering and tongue-tied. I arrested him at once, of course. I knew he was probably innocent, but a basic rule is to grab the first man on the scene of crime, especially if he happens to be a servant. But we let him go after a beating. There was nothing much he could tell us, and he had a sound alibi.

'The axe with which the rani had been killed must have been a small woodcutter's axe—so we deduced from the wound. We couldn't find the weapon. It might have been used by a man or a woman, and there were several of both sexes who had a grudge against the rani. There were bazaar rumours that she had been supplementing her income by trafficking in young women—she had the necessary connections. There were also rumours that she possessed vast wealth, and that it was stored away in her godowns. We did not find any treasure. There were so many rumours darting about like battered shuttlecocks that I decided to stop wasting my time in trying to follow them up. Instead, I restricted my enquiries to those people who had been close to the rani—either in their personal relationships or in actual physical proximity.

'To begin, there was Mr Kapur, a wealthy businessman from Bombay who had a house in Panauli. He was supposed to be an old admirer of the rani's. I discovered that he had occasionally lent her money, and that, in spite of his professed friendship for her, had charged a high rate of interest. Then, with, there were immediate neighbours—an American missionary and his wife— who had been trying to convert the rani to Christianity; an English spinster of seventy who made no secret of the fact that she and the rani had hated each other with great enthusiasm; a local councillor and his family who did not get on well with their aristocratic neighbour; and a tailor, who kept his shop close by. None of these people had any powerful motive for killing the rani—or none that I could discover. But the tailor's daughter interested me.

'Her name was Kusum. She was twelve or thirteen years old—a thin, dark girl with lovely black eyes and a swift, disarming smile. While I was making my routine enquiries in the vicinity of the rani's house, I noticed that the girl always tried to avoid me. When I questioned her about the rani, and about her own movements on the day of the crime, she pretended to be very vague and stupid.

'But I could see she was not stupid, and I became convinced that she knew something unusual about the rani. She might even know something about the murder. She could have been protecting someone, and was afraid to tell me what she knew. Often, when I spoke to her of the violence of the rani's death, I saw fear in her eyes. I began to think the girl's life might be in danger, and I had a close watch kept on her. I liked her. I liked her youth and freshness, and the innocence and wonder in her eyes. I spoke to her whenever I could, kindly and paternally, and though I knew she rather liked me and found me amusing—the ups and downs of Panauli always left me panting for breath—and though I could see that she *wanted* to tell me something, she always held back at the last moment.

'Then, one afternoon, while I was in the rani's house going through her effects, I saw something glistening in a narrow crack near the doorstep. I would not have noticed it if the sun had not been pouring through the window, glinting off the little object. I stooped and picked up a piece of glass. It was part of a broken bangle.

'I turned the fragment over in my hand. There was something familiar about its colour and design. Didn't Kusum wear similar glass bangles? I went to look for the girl but she was not in her father's shop. I was told that she had gone down the hill, to gather firewood.

'I decided to take the narrow path down the hill. It went round some rocks and cacti, and then disappeared into a forest of oak trees. I found Kusum sitting at the edge of the forest, a bundle of twigs beside her.

"You are always wandering alone," I said. "Don't you feel afraid?"

"It is safer when I am alone," she replied. "Nobody comes here."

'I glanced quickly at the bangles on her wrist, and noticed that their colour matched that of the broken piece. I held out the bit of broken glass and said, "I found it in the rani's house. It must have fallen..."

'She did not wait for me to finish what I was saying. With a look of terror, she sprang up from the grass and fled into the forest.

'I was completely taken aback. I had not expected such a reaction. Of what significance was the broken bangle? I hurried after the girl, slipping on the smooth pine needles that covered the slopes. I was searching amongst the trees when I heard someone sobbing behind me. When I turned round, I saw the girl standing on a boulder, facing the slope towards me.

'When Kusum saw me staring at her, she raised the axe and rushed down the slope towards me.

'I was too bewildered to be able to do anything but stare open-mouthed as she rushed at me with the axe. The impetus of her run would have brought her right against me, and the axe, coming down, would probably have crushed my skull, thick though it is. But while she was still six feet from me, the axe flew out of her hands. It sprang into the air as though it had a life of its own and came curving towards me.

'In spite of my weight, I moved swiftly aside. The axe grazed my shoulder and sank into the soft bark of the tree behind me and Kusum dropped at my feet, weeping hysterically.'

Inspector Keemat Lal paused in order to replenish his glass. He took a long pull at the beer, and the froth glistened on his moustache.

'And then what happened?' I prompted him.

'Perhaps it could only have happened in India—and to a person like me,' he said. 'This sudden compassion for the person you are supposed to destroy. Instead of being furious and outraged, instead of seizing the girl and marching her off to the police station, I stroked her head and said silly comforting things.'

'And she told you that she had killed the rani?'

'She told me how the rani had called her to her house and given her tea and sweets. Mr Kapur had been there. After some time he began stroking Kusum's arms and squeezing her knees. She had drawn away, but Kapur kept pawing her. The rani was telling Kusum not to be afraid, that no harm would come to her. Kusum slipped away from the man and made a rush for the door. The rani caught her by the shoulders and pushed her back into the room. The rani was getting angry. Kusum saw the axe lying in a corner of the room. She seized it, raised it above her head and threatened Kapur. The man realized that he had gone too far, and valuing his neck, backed away. But the rani, in a great rage, sprang at the girl. And Kusum, in desperation and panic, brought the axe down upon the rani's head.

'The rani fell to the ground. Without waiting to see what Kapur might do, Kusum fled from the house. Her bangle must have broken when she stumbled against the door. She ran into the forest and, after concealing the axe amongst some tall ferns, lay weeping on the grass until it grew dark. But such was her nature, and such the resilience of youth, that she recovered sufficiently to be able to return home looking her normal self. And during the following days, she managed to remain silent about the whole business.'

'What did you do about it?' I asked

Keemat Lal looked me straight in my beery eye.

'Nothing,' he said. 'I did absolutely nothing. I couldn't have the girl put away in a remand home. It would have crushed her spirit.'

'And what about Kapur?'

'Oh, he had his own reasons for remaining quiet, as you may guess. No, the case was closed—or perhaps I should say the file was put in my pending tray. My promotion, too, went into the pending tray.'

'It didn't turn out very well for you,' I said.

'No. Here I am in Shahpur, and still an inspector. But, tell me, what would you have done if you had been in my place?'

I considered his question carefully for a moment or two, then said, 'I suppose it would have depended on how much sympathy the girl evoked in me. Had she killed an innocent...'

'Then you would have put your personal feelings above your duty to uphold the law?'

'Yes. But I would not have made a very good policeman.'

'Exactly.'

'Still, it's a pity that Kapur got off so easily.'

'There was no alternative if I was to let the girl go. But he didn't get off altogether. He found himself in trouble later on for swindling some manufacturing concern, and went to jail for a couple of years.'

'And the girl—did you see her again?'

'Well, before I was transferred from Panauli, I saw her occasionally on the road. She was usually on her way to school. She would greet me with folded hands, and call me uncle.'

The beer bottles were all empty, and Inspector Keemat Lal got up to leave. His final words to me were, 'I should never have been a policeman.'

THE THIEF'S STORY

I was still a thief when I met Romi. And though I was only fifteen years old, I was an experienced and fairly successful hand. Romi was watching a wrestling match when I approached him. He was about twenty-five and he looked easy-going, kind, and simple enough for my purpose. I was sure I would be able to win the young man's confidence.

'You look a bit of a wrestler yourself,' I said. There's nothing like flattery to break the ice!

'So do you,' he replied, which put me off for a moment because at that time I was rather thin and bony.

'Well,' I said modestly, 'I do wrestle a bit.'

'What's your name?'

'Hari Singh,' I lied. I took a new name every month, which kept me ahead of the police and former employers.

After these formalities Romi confined himself to commenting on the wrestlers, who were grunting, gasping, and heaving each other about. When he walked away, I followed him casually.

'Hello again,' I said.

I gave him my most appealing smile. 'I want to work for you,' I said.

'But I can't pay you anything, not for some time, anyway.'

I thought that over for a minute. Perhaps I had misjudged my man. 'Can you feed me?' I asked.

'Can you cook?'

'I can cook,' I lied again.

'If you can cook, then maybe I can feed you.'

The Thief's Story

He took me to his room over the Delhi Sweet Shop and told me I could sleep on the balcony. But the meal I cooked that night must have been terrible because Romi gave it to a stray dog and told me to be off.

But I just hung around, smiling in my most appealing way, and he couldn't help laughing.

Later he said never mind, he'd teach me to cook. He also taught me to write my name and said he would soon teach me to write whole sentences and to add figures. I was grateful. I knew that once I could write like an educated person, there would be no limit to what I could achieve.

It was quite pleasant working for Romi. I made tea in the morning and then took my time buying the day's supplies, usually making a profit of two or three rupees. I think he knew I made a little money this way, but he didn't seem to mind.

Romi made money by fits and starts. He would borrow one week, lend the next. He kept worrying about his next cheque, but as soon as it arrived he would go out and celebrate. He wrote for the Delhi and Bombay magazines—a strange way to make a living.

One evening he came home with a small bundle of notes, saying he had just sold a book to a publisher. That night I saw him put the money in an envelope and tuck it under the mattress.

I had been working for Romi for almost a month and, apart from cheating on the shopping, had not done anything big in my real line of work. I had every opportunity of doing so. I could come and go as I pleased, and Romi was the most trusting person I had ever met.

That was why it was so difficult to rob him. It was easy for me to rob a greedy man. But robbing a nice man could be a problem. And if he doesn't notice he's being robbed, then all the spice goes out of the undertaking!

Well, it's time I got down to some real work, I told myself. If I don't take the money, he'll only waste it on his so-called friends. After all, he doesn't even give me a salary.

Romi was sleeping peacefully. A beam of moonlight reached over the balcony and fell on his bed. I sat on the floor, considering the situation. If I took the money, I could catch the 10.30 express to Lucknow. Slipping out of my blanket, I crept over to the bed.

My hand slid under the mattress, searching for the notes. When I found the packet, I drew it out without a sound. Romi sighed in his sleep and turned on his side. Startled, I moved quickly out of the room.

Once on the road, I began to run. I had the money stuffed into a vest pocket under my shirt. When I'd gotten some distance from Romi's place, I slowed to a walk and, taking the envelope from my pocket, counted the money. Seven hundred rupees in fifties. I could live like a prince for a week or two!

When I reached the station, I did not stop at the ticket office (I had never bought a ticket in my life) but dashed straight on to the platform. The Lucknow Express was just moving out. The train had still to pick up speed and I should have been able to jump into one of the compartments, but I hesitated—for some reason I can't explain—and I lost my chance to get away.

When the train had gone, I found myself standing alone on the deserted platform. I had no idea where to spend the night. I had no friends, believing that friends were more trouble than help. And I did not want to arouse curiosity by staying at one of the small hotels nearby. The only person I knew really well was the man I had robbed. Leaving the station, I walked slowly through the bazaar.

In my short career, I had made a study of people's faces after they had discovered the loss of their valuables. The greedy showed panic; the rich showed anger; the poor, resignation. But I knew that Romi's face when he discovered the theft would show only a touch of sadness—not for the loss of money, but for the loss of trust.

The night was chilly—November nights can be cold in

northern India—and a shower of rain added to my discomfort. I sat down in the shelter of the clock tower. A few beggars and vagrants lay beside me, rolled up tight in their blankets. The clock showed midnight. I felt for the notes, they were soaked through.

Romi's money. In the morning, he would probably have given me five rupees to go to the movies, but now I had it all—no more cooking meals, running to the bazaar, or learning to write sentences.

Sentences! I had forgotten about them in the excitement of the theft. Writing complete sentences, I knew, could one day bring me more than a few hundred rupees. It was a simple matter to steal. But to be a really big man, a clever and respected man, was something else. I should go back to Romi, I told myself, if only to learn to read and write.

I hurried back to the room feeling very nervous, for it is much easier to steal something than to return it undetected.

I opened the door quietly, then stood in the doorway in clouded moonlight. Romi was still asleep. I crept to the head of the bed, and my hand came up with the packet of notes. I felt his breath on my hand. I remained still for a few moments. Then my fingers found the edge of the mattress, and I slipped the money beneath it.

I awoke late the next morning to find that Romi had already made the tea. He stretched out a hand to me. There was a fifty-rupee note between his fingers. My heart sank.

'I made some money yesterday,' he said. 'Now I'll be able to pay you regularly.'

My spirits rose. But when I took the note, I noticed that it was still wet from the night's rain.

So he knew what I'd done. But neither his lips nor his eyes revealed anything.

'Today we'll start writing sentences,' he said.

I smiled at Romi in my most appealing way. And the smile came by itself, without any effort.

THE FIGHT

Ranji had been less than a month in Rajpur when he discovered the pool in the forest. It was the height of summer, and his school had not yet opened and, having as yet made no friends in this semi-hill station, he wandered about a good deal by himself into the hills and forests that stretched away interminably on all sides of the town. It was hot, very hot, at that time of year, and Ranji walked about in his vest and shorts, his brown feet white with the chalky dust that flew up from the ground. The earth was parched, the grass brown, the trees listless, hardly stirring, waiting for a cool wind or a refreshing shower of rain.

It was on such a day—a hot, tired day—that Ranji found the pool in the forest. The water had a gentle translucency, and you could see the smooth round pebbles at the bottom of the pool. A small stream emerged from a cluster of rocks to feed the pool. During the monsoon, this stream would be a gushing torrent, cascading down from the hills, but during the summer it was barely a trickle. The rocks, however, held the water in the pool, and it did not dry up like the pools in the plains.

When Ranji saw the pool, he did not hesitate to get into it. He had often gone swimming, alone or with friends, when he had lived with his parents in a thirsty town in the middle of the Rajputana desert. There, he had known only sticky, muddy pools, where buffaloes wallowed and women washed clothes. He had never seen a pool like this—so clean and cold and inviting. He threw off all his clothes, as he had done when he went swimming in the plains, and leapt into the water. His limbs were supple, free of any fat, and his dark body glistened in patches of sunlit water.

The next day he came again to quench his body in the cool waters of the forest pool. He was there for almost an hour, sliding in and out of the limpid green water, or lying stretched out on the smooth yellow rocks in the shade of broad-leaved sal trees. It was while he lay thus, naked on a rock, that he noticed another boy standing a little distance away, staring at him in a rather hostile manner. The other boy was a little older than Ranji, taller, thickset, with a broad nose and thick, red lips. He had only just noticed Ranji, and he stood at the edge of the pool, wearing a pair of bathing shorts, waiting for Ranji to explain himself.

When Ranji did not say anything, the other called out, 'What are you doing here, mister?'

Ranji, who was prepared to be friendly, was taken aback at the hostility of the other's tone.

'I am swimming,' he replied. 'Why don't you join me?'

'I always swim alone,' said the other. 'This is my pool, I did not invite you here. And why are you not wearing clothes?'

'It is not your business if I do not wear clothes. I have nothing to be ashamed of.'

'You skinny fellow, put on your clothes.'

'Fat fool, take yours off.'

This was too much for the stranger to tolerate. He strode up to Ranji, who still sat on the rock and, planting his broad feet firmly on the sand, said (as though this would settle the matter once, and for all), 'Don't you know I am a Punjabi? I do not take replies from villagers like you!'

'So you like to fight with villagers?' said Ranji. 'Well, I am not a villager. I am a Rajput!'

'I am a Punjabi!'

'I am a Rajput!'

They had reached an impasse. One had said he was a Punjabi,

the other had proclaimed himself a Rajput. There was little else that could be said.

'You understand that I am a Punjabi?' said the stranger feeling that perhaps this information had not penetrated Ranji's head.

'I have heard you say it three times,' replied Ranji.

'Then why are you not running away?'

'I am waiting for *you* to run away!'

'I will have to beat you,' said the stranger, assuming a violent attitude, showing Ranji the palm of his hand.

'I am waiting to see you do it,' said Ranji.

'You will see me do it,' said the other boy.

Ranji waited. The other boy made a strange, hissing sound. They stared at each other in the eye for almost a minute. Then the Punjabi boy slapped Ranji across the face with all the force he could muster. Ranji staggered, feeling quite dizzy. There were thick red finger marks on his cheek.

'There you are!' exclaimed his assailant. 'Will you be off now?'

For answer, Ranji swung his arm up and pushed a hard, bony fist into the other's face.

And then they were at each other's throats, swaying on the rock, tumbling on the sand, rolling over and over, their legs and arms locked in a desperate, violent struggle. Gasping and cursing, clawing and slapping, they rolled right into the shallows of the pool.

Even in the water the fight continued as, spluttering and covered with mud, they groped for each other's head and throat. But after five minutes of frenzied, unscientific struggle, neither boy had emerged victorious. Their bodies heaving with exhaustion, they stood back from each other, making tremendous efforts to speak.

'Now—now do you realize—I am a Punjabi?' gasped the stranger.

'Do you know I am a Rajput?' said Ranji with difficulty.

They gave a moment's consideration to each other's answers, and in that moment of silence there was only their heavy breathing and the rapid beating of their hearts.

'Then you will not leave the pool?' said the Punjabi boy.

'I will not leave it,' said Ranji.

'Then we shall have to continue the fight,' said the other.

'All right,' said Ranji.

But neither boy moved, neither took the initiative.

The Punjabi boy had an inspiration.

'We will continue the fight tomorrow,' he said. 'If you dare to come here again tomorrow, we will continue this fight, and I will not show you mercy as I have done today.'

'I will come tomorrow,' said Ranji. 'I will be ready for you.'

They turned from each other then and, going to their respective rocks, put on their clothes, and left the forest by different routes.

When Ranji got home, he found it difficult to explain the cuts and bruises that showed on his face, legs and arms. It was difficult to conceal the fact that he had been in an unusually violent fight, and his mother insisted on his staying at home for the rest of the day. That evening, though, he slipped out of the house and went to the bazaar, where he found comfort and solace in a bottle of vividly coloured lemonade and a banana leaf full of hot, sweet jalebis. He had just finished the lemonade when he saw his adversary coming down the road. His first impulse was to turn away and look elsewhere, his second to throw the lemonade bottle at his enemy. But he did neither of these things. Instead, he stood his ground and scowled at his passing adversary. And the Punjabi boy said nothing either, but scowled back with equal ferocity.

The next day was as hot as the previous one. Ranji felt weak and lazy and not at all eager for a fight. His body was stiff and sore after the previous day's encounter. But he could not refuse the challenge. Not to turn up at the pool would be an acknowledgement of defeat. From the way he felt just then, he knew he would be beaten in another fight. But he could not acquiesce in his own defeat. He must defy his enemy to the last, or outwit him, for only then could he gain his respect. If he surrendered now, he would be beaten for all time; but to fight and be beaten today left him free to fight and be beaten again. As long as he fought, he had a right to the pool in the forest.

He was half hoping that the Punjabi boy would have forgotten the challenge, but these hopes were dashed when he saw his opponent sitting, stripped to the waist, on a rock on the other side of the pool. The Punjabi boy was rubbing oil on his body, massaging it into his broad thighs. He saw Ranji beneath the sal trees, and called a challenge across the waters of the pool.

'Come over on this side and fight!' he shouted.

But Ranji was not going to submit to any conditions laid down by his opponent.

'Come *this* side and fight!' he shouted back with equal vigour.

'Swim across and fight me here!' called the other. 'Or perhaps you cannot swim the length of this pool?'

But Ranji could have swum the length of the pool a dozen times without tiring, and here he would show the Punjabi boy his superiority. So, slipping out of his vest and shorts, he dived straight into the water, cutting through it like a knife, and surfaced with hardly a splash. The Punjabi boy's mouth hung open in amazement.

'You can dive!' he exclaimed.

'It is easy,' said Ranji, treading water, waiting for a further challenge. 'Can't you dive?'

'No,' said the other. 'I jump straight in. But if you will tell me how, I will make a dive.'

'It is easy,' said Ranji. 'Stand on the rock, stretch your arms out and allow your head to displace your feet.'

The Punjabi boy stood up, stiff and straight, stretched out his arms, and threw himself into the water. He landed flat on his belly with a crash that sent the birds screaming out of the trees.

Ranji dissolved into laughter.

'Are you trying to empty the pool?' he asked, as the Punjabi boy came to the surface, spouting water like a small whale.

'Wasn't it good?' asked the boy, evidently proud of his feat.

'Not very good,' said Ranji. 'You should have more practice. See, I will do it again.'

And, pulling himself up on a rock, he executed another perfect dive. The other boy waited for him to come up, but, swimming under water, Ranji circled him and came upon him from behind.

'How did you do that?' asked the astonished youth.

'Can't you swim under water?' asked Ranji.

'No, but I will try it.'

The Punjabi boy made a tremendous effort to plunge to the bottom of the pool and indeed he thought he had gone right down, though his bottom, like a duck's, remained above the surface.

Ranji, however, did not discourage him.

'It was not bad,' he said. 'But you need a lot of practice.'

'Will you teach me?' asked his enemy.

'If you like, I will teach you.'

'You must teach me. If you do not teach me, I will beat you. Will you come here every day and teach me?'

'If you like,' said Ranji. They had pulled themselves out of the water, and were sitting side by side on a smooth grey rock.

'My name is Suraj,' said the Punjabi boy. 'What is yours?'

'It is Ranji.'

'I am strong, am I not?' asked Suraj, bending his arms so that a ball of muscles stood up stretching the white of his flesh.

'You are strong,' said Ranji. 'You are a real pehalwan.'

'One day I will be the world's champion wrestler,' said Suraj, slapping his thighs, which shook with the impact of his hand. He looked critically at Ranji's hard, thin body. 'You are quite strong yourself,' he conceded. 'But you are too bony. I know you people do not eat enough. You must come and have your food with me. I drink one seer of milk of every day. We have got our own cow! Be my friend, and I will make you a pehalwan like me! I know—if you teach me to dive and swim under water, I will make you a pehalwan! That is fair, isn't it?'

'That is fair!' said Ranji, although he doubted he was getting the better of the exchange.

Suraj put his arm around the younger boy and said, 'We are friends now, yes?'

They looked at each other with honest, unflinching eyes, and in that moment love and understanding were born.

'We are friends,' said Ranji.

The birds had settled again on their branches, and the pool was quiet and limpid in the shade of the sal trees.

'It is our pool,' said Suraj. 'Nobody else can come here without our permission. Who would dare?'

'Who would dare?' said Ranji, smiling with the knowledge that he had won the day.

FAIRY GLEN PALACE

The old bridle path from Rajpur to Mussoorie passed through Fosterganj at a height of about five thousand feet. In the old days, before the motor road was built, this was the only road to the hill station. You could ride up on a pony, or walk, or be carried in a basket (if you were a child) or in a doolie (if you were a lady or an invalid). The doolie was a cross between a hammock, stretcher and sedan chair, if you can imagine such a contraption. It was borne aloft by two perspiring bearers. Sometimes they sat down to rest, and dropped you unceremoniously. I have a picture of my grandmother being borne uphill in a doolie, and she looks petrified. There was an incident in which a doolie, its occupant, and two bearers, all went over a cliff just before Fosterganj, and perished in the fall. Sometimes you can see the ghost of this poor lady being borne uphill by two phantom bearers.

Fosterganj has its ghosts, of course. And they are something of a distraction.

Writing is my vocation, and I have always tried to follow the apostolic maxim, 'Study to be quiet and to mind your own business'. But in small-town India one is constantly drawn into other people's business, just as they are drawn towards yours. In Fosterganj it was quiet enough, there were few people; there was no excuse for shirking work. But tales of haunted houses and fairy-infested forests have always intrigued me, and when I heard that the ruined palace halfway down to Rajpur was a place to be avoided after dark, it was natural for me to start taking my evening walks in its direction.

Fairy Glen was its name. It had been built on the lines of a Swiss or French chalet, with numerous turrets decorating its many wings—a huge, rambling building, two-storeyed, with numerous balconies and cornices and windows; a hodgepodge of architectural styles, a wedding cake of a palace, built to satisfy the whims and fancies of its late owner, the Raja of Ranipur, a small state near the Nepal border. Maintaining this ornate edifice must have been something of a nightmare, and the present heirs had quite given up on it, for bits of the roof were missing, some windows were without panes, doors had developed cracks, and what had once been a garden was now a small jungle.

Apparently, there was no one living there anymore, no sign of a caretaker. I had walked past the wrought-iron gate several times without seeing any signs of life, apart from a large grey cat sunning itself outside a broken window.

Then, one evening, walking up from Rajpur, I was caught in a storm.

A wind had sprung up, bringing with it dark, overburdened clouds. Heavy drops of rain were followed by hailstones bouncing off the stony path. Gusts of wind rushed through the oaks, and leaves and small branches were soon swirling through the air. I was still a couple of miles from the Fosterganj bazaar, and I did not fancy sheltering under a tree, as flashes of lightning were beginning to light up the darkening sky. Then I found myself outside the gate of the abandoned palace.

Outside the gate stood an old sentry box. No one had stood sentry in it for years. It was a good place in which to shelter. But I hesitated because a large bird was perched on the gate, seemingly oblivious to the rain that was still falling.

It looked like a crow or a raven, but it was much bigger than either—in fact, twice the size of a crow, but having all the features of one—and when a flash of lightning lit up the gate, it gave a squawk, opened its enormous wings and took off, flying in the direction of the oak forest. I hadn't seen such a bird before—there was something dark and malevolent and almost supernatural about it. But it had gone, and I darted into the sentry box without further delay.

I had been standing there some ten minutes, wondering when the rain was going to stop, when I heard someone running down the road. As he approached, I could see that he was just a boy, probably eleven or twelve, but in the dark I could not make out his features. He came up to the gate, lifted the latch, and was about to go in when he saw me in the sentry box.

'Kaun? Who are you?' he asked, first in Hindi, then in English. He did not appear to be in any way anxious or alarmed.

'Just sheltering from the rain,' I said. 'I live in the bazaar.'

He took a small torch from his pocket and shone it in my face.

'Yes, I have seen you there. A tourist.'

'A writer. I stay in places, I don't just pass through.'

'Do you want to come in?'

I hesitated. It was still raining and the roof of the sentry box was leaking badly.

'Do you live here?' I asked.

'Yes, I am the raja's nephew. I live here with my mother. Come in.'

He took me by the hand and led me through the gate. His hand was quite rough and heavy for an eleven- or twelve-year-old. Instead of walking with me to the front steps and entrance of the old palace, he led me around to the rear of the building, where a faint light glowed in a mullioned window, and in its light I saw that he had a very fresh and pleasant face—a face as yet untouched by the trials of life.

Instead of knocking on the door, he tapped on the window.

'Only strangers knock on the door,' he said. 'When I tap on the window, my mother knows it's me.'

'That's clever of you,' I said.

He tapped again, and the door was opened by an unusually tall woman wearing a kind of loose, flowing gown that looked strange in that place, and on her. The light was behind her, and I couldn't see her face until we had entered the room. When she turned to me, I saw that she had a long reddish scar running down one side of her face. Even so, there was a certain, hard beauty in her appearance.

'Make some tea—Mother,' said the boy rather brusquely.

'And something to eat. I'm hungry. Sir, will you have something?' He looked enquiringly at me. The light from a kerosene lamp fell full on his face. He was wide-eyed, full-lipped, smiling; only his voice seemed rather mature for one so young. And he spoke like someone much older, and with an almost unsettling sophistication.

'Sit down, sir,' he led me to a chair, made me comfortable.

'You are not too wet, I hope?'

'No, I took shelter before the rain came down too heavily. But you are wet, you'd better change.'

'It doesn't bother me.' And after a pause, 'Sorry there is no electricity. Bills haven't been paid for years.'

'Is this your place?'

'No, we are only caretakers. Poor relations, you might say. The palace has been in dispute for many years. The raja and his brothers keep fighting over it, and meanwhile it is slowly falling down. The lawyers are happy. Perhaps I should study and become a lawyer someday.'

'Do you go to school?'

'Sometimes.'

'How old are you?'

'Quite old, I'm not sure. Mother, how old am I?' he asked, as the tall woman returned with cups of tea and a plate full of biscuits.

She hesitated, gave him a puzzled look. 'Don't you know? It's on your certificate.'

'I've lost the certificate.'

'No, I've kept it safely.' She looked at him intently, placed a hand on his shoulder, then turned to me and said, 'He is twelve,' with a certain finality.

We finished our tea. It was still raining.

'It will rain all night,' said the boy. 'You had better stay here.'

'It will inconvenience you.'

'No, it won't. There are many rooms. If you do not mind the darkness. Come, I will show you everything. And meanwhile my mother will make some dinner. Very simple food, I hope you won't mind.'

The boy took me around the old palace, if you could still call it that. He led the way with a candle-holder from which a large candle threw our exaggerated shadows on the walls.

'What's your name?' I asked, as he led me into what must have been a reception room, still crowded with ornate furniture and bric-a-brac.

'Bhim,' he said. 'But everyone calls me Lucky.'

'And are you lucky?'

He shrugged. 'Don't know...' Then he smiled up at me. 'Maybe you'll bring me luck.'

We walked further into the room. Large oil paintings hung from the walls, gathering mould. Some were portraits of royalty, kings and queens of another era, wearing decorative headgear, strange uniforms, the women wrapped in jewellery—more jewels than garments, it seemed—and sometimes accompanied by children who were also weighed down by excessive clothing. A young man sat on a throne, his lips curled in a sardonic smile.

'My grandfather,' said Bhim.

He led me into a large bedroom taken up by a four-poster bed which had probably seen several royal couples copulating upon it. It looked cold and uninviting, but Bhim produced a voluminous razai from a cupboard and assured me that it would be warm and quite luxurious, as it had been his grandfather's.

'And when did your grandfather die?' I asked.

'Oh, fifty-sixty years ago, it must have been.'

'In this bed, I suppose.'

'No, he was shot accidentally while out hunting. They said it was an accident. But he had enemies.'

'Kings have enemies... And this was the royal bed?'

He gave me a sly smile, not so innocent after all. 'Many women slept in it. He had many queens.'

'And concubines.'

'What are concubines?'

'Unofficial queens.'

'Yes, those too.'

A worldly-wise boy of twelve...

I did not feel like sleeping in that room, with its musty old draperies and paint peeling off the walls. A trickle of water from the ceiling fell down the back of my shirt and made me shiver.

'The roof is leaking,' I said. 'Maybe I'd better go home.'

'You can't go now, it's very late. And that leopard has been seen again.'

He fetched a china bowl from the dressing-table and placed it on the floor to catch the trickle from the ceiling. In another corner of the room a metal bucket was receiving a steady patter from another leak.

'The palace is leaking everywhere,' said Bhim cheerfully. 'This is the only dry room.'

He took me by the hand and led me back to his own quarters. I was surprised, again, by how heavy and rough his hand was for a boy, and presumed that he did a certain amount of manual work such as chopping wood for a daily fire. In winter the building would be unbearably cold.

His mother gave us a satisfying meal, considering the ingredients at her disposal were somewhat limited. Once again, I tried to get away. But only half-heartedly. The boy intrigued me, so did his mother; so did the rambling old palace; and the rain persisted.

Bhim the Lucky took me to my room, waited with the

guttering candle till I had removed my shoes, handed me a pair of very large pyjamas.

'Royal pyjamas,' he said with a smile.

I got into them and floated around.

'Before you go,' I said. 'I might want to visit the bathroom in the night.'

'Of course, sir. It's close by.' He opened a door, and beyond it I saw a dark passage. 'Go a little way, and there's a door on the left. I'm leaving an extra candle and matches on the dressing table.'

He put the lighted candle he was carrying on the table, and left the room without a light. Obviously he knew his way about in the dark. His footsteps receded, and I was left alone with the sound of raindrops pattering on the roof and a loose sheet of corrugated tin roofing flapping away in a wind that had now sprung up.

It was a summer's night, and I had no need of blankets, so I removed my shoes and jacket and lay down on the capacious bed, wondering if I should blow the candle out or allow it to burn as long as it lasted.

Had I been in my own room, I would have been reading—a Conrad or a Chekhov or some other classic—because at night I turn to the classics—but here there was no light and nothing to read.

I got up and blew the candle out. I might need it later on. Restless, I prowled around the room in the dark, banging into chairs and footstools. I made my way to the window and drew the curtains aside. Some light filtered into the room because behind the clouds there was a moon, and it had been a full moon the night before.

I lay back on the bed. It wasn't very comfortable. It was a box-bed, of the sort that had only just begun to become popular in households with small bedrooms. This one had been around for some time—no doubt a very early version of its type—and although it was covered with a couple of thick mattresses, the woodwork appeared to have warped because it creaked loudly whenever I shifted my position. The boards no longer fitted properly. Either that, or the box-bed had been overstuffed with all sorts of things.

After some time I settled into one position and dozed off for a while, only to be awakened by the sound of someone screaming somewhere in the building. My hair stood on end. The screaming continued, and I wondered if I should get up to investigate. Then suddenly it stopped—broke off in the middle as though it had been muffled by a hand or piece of cloth.

There was a tapping at the pane of the big French window in front of the bed. Probably the branch of a tree, swaying in the wind. But then there was a screech, and I sat up in bed. Another screech, and I was out of it.

I went to the window and pressed my face to the glass.

The big black bird—the bird I had seen when taking shelter in the sentry box—was sitting, or rather squatting, on the boundary wall, facing me. The moon, now visible through the clouds, fell full upon it. I had never seen a bird like it before. Crow-like, but heavily built, like a turkey, its beak that of a bird of prey, its talons those of a vulture. I stepped back, and closed the heavy curtains, shutting out the light but also shutting out the image of that menacing bird.

Returning to the bed, I just sat there for a while, wondering if I should get up and leave. The rain had lessened. But the luminous dial of my watch showed it was two in the morning. No time for a stroll in the dark—not with a man-eating leopard in the vicinity.

Then I heard the shriek again. It seemed to echo through the building. It may have been the bird, but to me it sounded all too human. There was silence for a long while after that. I lay back on the bed and tried to sleep. But it was even more uncomfortable than before. Perhaps the wood had warped too much during the monsoon, I thought, and the lid of the old box-bed did not fit properly. Maybe I could push it back into its correct position; then perhaps I could get some sleep.

So I got up again, and after fumbling around in the dark for a few minutes, found the matches and lit the candle.

Then I removed the sheets from the bed and pulled away the two mattresses. The cover of the box-bed lay exposed. And a hand protruded from beneath the lid. It was not a living hand. It was a skeletal hand, fleshless, brittle. But there was a ring on one finger, an opal still clinging to the bone of a small index finger. It glowed faintly in the candlelight.

Shaking a little (for I am really something of a coward, though an inquisitive one), I lifted the lid of the box-bed. Laid out on a pretty counterpane was a skeleton. A bundle of bones, but still clothed in expensive-looking garments. One hand gripped the side of the box-bed; the hand that had kept it from shutting properly. I dropped the lid of the box-bed and ran from the room—only to blunder into a locked door. Someone, presumably the boy, had locked me into the bedroom.

I banged on the door and shouted, but no one heard me.

No one came running. I went to the large French window, but it was firmly fastened, it probably hadn't been opened for many years.

Then I remembered the passageway leading to the bathroom. The boy had pointed it out to me. Possibly there was a way out from there.

There was. It was an old door that opened easily, and I stepped out into the darkness, finding myself entangled in a creeper that grew against the wall. From its cloying fragrance I recognized it as wisteria.

A narrow path led to a wicket gate at the end of the building. I found my way out of the grounds and back on the familiar public road. The old palace loomed out of the darkness. I turned my back on it and set off for home, my little room above Hassan's bakery.

Nothing happens in Fosterganj, I told myself. But something had happened in that old palace...

'What did you want to go there for?' asked Hassan, when I knocked on his door at the crack of dawn.

'It was raining heavily, and I stopped near the gate to take shelter. A boy invited me in, his mother gave me something to eat, and I ended up spending the night in the raja's bedroom.' I said nothing about screams in the night or the skeleton in the bed. Hassan presented me with a bun and a glass of hot sweet tea.

'Nobody goes there,' he said. 'The place has a bad name.'

'And why's that?'

'The old raja was a bad man. Tortured his wives, or so it was said.'

'And what happened to him?'

'Got killed in a hunting accident, in the jungles next to Bijnor. He went after a tiger, but the tiger got to him first. Bit his head off! Everyone was pleased. His younger brother inherited the palace, but he never comes here. I think he still lives somewhere near the Nepal border.'

'And the people who still live in the palace?'

'Poor relations, I think. Offspring from one of the raja's wives or concubines—no one quite knows, or even cares. We don't see much of them, and they keep to themselves. But people avoid the place, they say it is still full of evil, haunted by the old scoundrel whose cruelty has left its mark on the walls... It should be pulled down!'

'It's falling down of its own accord,' I said. 'Most of it is already a ruin.'

THE LAST TIGER

On the left bank of the Ganga, where it emerges from the Himalayan foothills, there is a long stretch of heavy forest. There are villages on the fringe of the forest, inhabited by bamboo cutters and farmers, but there are few signs of commerce or religion. Hunters, however, have found it an ideal hunting ground over the last seventy years, and as a result the animals are not as numerous as they used to be. The trees, too, have been disappearing slowly; and, as the forest recedes, the animals lose their food and shelter and move on, further into the foothills. Slowly, they are being denied the right to live.

Only the elephants could cross the river. And two years ago, when a large area of forest was cleared to make way for a refugee resettlement camp, a herd of elephants—finding their favourite food, the green shoots of the bamboo, in short supply—waded across the river. They crashed through the suburbs of Haridwar, knocked down a factory wall, plucked away several tin roofs, held up a train, and left a trail of devastation in their wake until they reached a new forest, still untouched, where they settled down to a new life—but an unsettled, wary life. Because, they did not know when men would appear again, with tractors and bulldozers and dynamite.

There was a time when this forest provided food and shelter for some thirty or forty tigers; but men in search of trophies shot them all, and today there remains only one old tiger in the jungle. Many hunters have tried to get him. But he is a wise and crafty old tiger who knows the ways of men, and he has so far survived all attempts on his life.

This is his story. It is also the story of the jungle.

❧

Although the tiger has passed the prime of his life, he has lost none of his majesty; his muscles ripple beneath the golden yellow of his coat, and he walks through the long grass with the confidence of one who knows that he is still king, even though his subjects are fewer. His great head pushes through the foliage, and it is only his tail, swinging high, that shows occasionally above the sea of grass.

He is heading for water, the only water in the forest (if you don't count the river, which is several miles away)—the water of a large jheel, which is almost a lake during the rainy season, but just a muddy marsh at this time of the year, in the late spring.

Here, at different times of the day and night, all the animals come to drink—the long-horned sambar deer, the delicate spotted chital, the swamp deer, the wolves and jackals, the wild boar, the panthers—and the tiger. Since the elephants have gone, the water is usually clear except when buffaloes from the nearest village come to wallow, and then it is very muddy. These buffaloes, though they are not wild, are not afraid of the panther or even of the tiger. They know the panther is afraid of their long horns and they know the tiger prefers the flesh of the deer.

Today, there are several sambar at the water's edge, but they do not stay long. The tiger is coming with the breeze, and there is no mistaking its strong feline odour. The deer hold their heads high for a few moments, their nostrils twitching, and then scatter into the forest, disappearing behind screens of leaf and bamboo.

When the tiger arrives, there is no other animal near the water. But the birds are still there. The egrets continue to wade in the shallows, and a kingfisher darts low over the water, dives suddenly, a flash of blue and gold, and makes off with a slim silver fish, which glistens in the sun like a polished gem. A long brown snake glides in amongst the water lilies and disappears beneath a fallen tree which lies rotting in the shallows.

The tiger waits in the shelter of a rock, his ears pricked up for the least unfamiliar sound; for he knows that it is often at this place that men lie up for him with guns; for they covet his beauty—they covet his stripes, and the gold of his body, and his fine teeth and his whiskers and his noble head. They would like to hang his pelt on a wall, and stick glass eyes in his head, and boast of their conquest over the king of the jungle.

The old tiger has been hunted before, and he does not usually show himself in the open during the day, but of late he has heard no guns, and if there were hunters around, you would have heard their guns (for a man with a gun cannot resist letting it off, even if it is only at a rabbit—or at another man). And, besides, the tiger is thirsty.

He is also feeling quite hot. It is March, and the shimmering dust-haze of summer has come early this year. Tigers—unlike other cats—are fond of water, and on a hot day will wallow for hours.

He walks into the water, in amongst the water lilies, and drinks slowly. He is seldom in a hurry when he eats or drinks. Other animals might bolt their food, but they are only other animals. A tiger has his dignity to preserve!

He raises his head and listens. One paw remains suspended in the air. A strange sound has come to him on the breeze, and he is wary of strange sounds. So he moves swiftly through the grass that borders the jheel, and climbs a hillock until he reaches his favourite rock. This rock is big enough to hide him and to give him shade. Anyone looking up from the jheel might think it strange that the rock has a round bump on the top. The bump is the tiger's head. He keeps it very still.

The sound he has heard is only the sound of a flute, sounding thin and reedy in the forest. It belongs to a boy, a slim brown boy who rides a buffalo. The boy blows vigorously on the flute, while another, slightly smaller boy, riding another buffalo, brings up the rear of the herd.

There are about eight buffaloes in the herd, and they belong to the families of Ramu and Shyam, the two Gujjar boys who are friends. The Gujjars are a caste who possess herds of buffaloes and earn their livelihood from the sale of milk and butter. The boys are about twelve years old, but they cannot tell you how many months past twelve, because in their village nobody thinks birthdays are important. They are almost the same age as the tiger, but he is old and experienced while they are still cubs.

※

The tiger has often seen them at the tank, and he is not worried. He knows the village people will bring him no harm as long as he leaves their buffaloes alone. Once, when he was younger and full of bravado, he had killed a buffalo—not because he was hungry but because he was young and wanted to test his strength—and after that the villagers had hunted him for days, with spears, bows and arrows, and an old muzzle-loader. Now he left the buffaloes alone, even though the deer in the forest were not as numerous as before.

The boys know that a tiger lives in the jungle, for they have often heard him roar, but they do not know that today he is so near to them.

The tiger gazes down from his rock, and the sight of eight fat black buffaloes does make him give a low, throaty moan. But the boys are there, and besides—a buffalo is not easy to kill.

He decides to move on and find a cool shady place in the heart of the jungle, where he can rest during the warm afternoon and be free of the flies and mosquitoes that swarm around in the vicinity of the tank. At night he will hunt.

With a lazy, half-humorous roar—'A—oonh!'—he gets up from his haunches and saunters off into the jungle.

Even the gentlest of a tiger's roars can be heard half a mile away, and the boys, who are barely fifty yards off, look up immediately.

'There he goes!' calls Ramu, taking the flute from his lips and pointing with it towards the hillock. He is not afraid, for he knows that an un-hunted and uninjured tiger is not aggressive. 'Did you see him?'

'I saw his tail, just before he disappeared. He's a big tiger!'

'Do not call him tiger. Call him Uncle, or Maharaj.'

'Oh, why?'

'Don't you know that it's unlucky to call a tiger a tiger? My father always told me so. But if you meet a tiger, and call him Uncle, he will leave you alone.'

'I'll try and remember that,' says Shyam.

※

The buffaloes are now well into the water, and some of them are lying down in the mud. Buffaloes love soft, wet mud and will wallow in it for hours. The more mud the better. Ramu, to avoid being dragged down into the mud with his buffalo, slips off its back and plunges into the water. Using an easy breaststroke, he swims across to a small islet covered with reeds and water lilies. Shyam is close behind him.

They lie down on their hard, flat stomachs, on a patch of grass, and allow the warm sun to beat down on their bare brown bodies. Ramu is the more knowledgeable boy, because he has been to Haridwar several times with his father. Shyam has never been out of the village.

Shyam says, 'The pool is not so deep this year.'

'We have had no rain since January,' says Ramu. 'If we do not get rain soon, the tank may dry up altogether.'

'And then what will we do?'

'We? There is a well in the village. But even that may dry up. My father told me that it failed once, just about the time I was born, and everyone had to walk ten miles to the river for water.'

'And what about the animals?'

'Some will stay here and die. Others will go to the river.

But there are too many people near the river now—not only temples, but houses and factories—and the animals stay away. And the trees have been cut, so that between the jungle and the river there is no place to hide. Animals are afraid of the open—they are afraid of men with guns.'

'Even at night?'

'At night men come in jeeps, with searchlights. They kill the deer for meat, and sell the skins of tigers and panthers.'

'I didn't know a tiger's skin was worth anything.'

'It is worth more than our skins,' says Ramu knowingly. 'It will fetch six hundred rupees. Who would pay that much for our skins?'

'Our fathers would.'

'True—if they had the money.'

'If my father sold his fields, he would get more than six hundred rupees.'

'True—but if he sold his fields, none of you would have anything to eat. A man needs land as much as a tiger needs a jungle.'

'True,' says Shyam. 'And that reminds me—my mother asked me to take some roots home.'

'I will help you.'

They wade into the jheel until the water is up to their waists, and begin pulling up water lilies by the root. The flower is beautiful but the villagers value the root more. When it is cooked, it makes a delicious and nourishing dish. The plant multiplies rapidly and is always in good supply. In the year when famine hit the village, it was only the root of the water lily that saved many from starvation.

When Shyam and Ramu have finished gathering roots, they emerge from the water and pass the time in wrestling with each other, slipping about in the soft mud which soon covers them from head to toe.

To get rid of the mud, they dive into the water again and

swim across to their buffaloes. Then, digging their heels into the thick hides of the buffaloes, the boys race them across the jheel, shouting and hollering so much that all the birds fly away in disgust, and the monkeys set up a shrill chattering of their own in the dhak trees.

In March, the twisted, leafless flame of the forest or dhak trees are ablaze with flaming scarlet and orange flowers.

It is evening, and the twilight is fading fast, when the buffalo herd finally wends its way homewards, to be greeted outside the village by the barking of dogs, the gurgle of hookah pipes, and the homely smell of cowdung smoke.

The tiger makes a kill that night. He approaches with the wind against him, and the unsuspecting spotted deer does not see him until it is too late. A blow on the deer's haunches from the tiger's paw brings it down, and then the great beast fastens onto the struggling deer's throat. It is all over in a few minutes. The tiger is too quick and strong, and the deer does not struggle for long.

The deer's life is over, but he has not lived in fear of death. It is only man's imagination and fear of the hereafter that makes him afraid of meeting death. In the jungle, sudden death appears at intervals. Wild creatures do not have to think about it, and so the sudden passing of one of their number due to the arrival of some flesh-eating animal is only a fleeting incident soon forgotten by the survivors.

The tiger feasts well, growling with pleasure as he eats, and then leaves the carcass in the jungle for the vultures and jackals. The old tiger never returns to the same deer's carcass, even if there is still some flesh on it. In the past, when he has done that, he has often found a man sitting in a tree over the kill, waiting for him with a rifle.

His belly full, the tiger comes to the edge of the forest, looks out across the wasteland out over the deep, singing river, at the twinkling lights of Haridwar on the opposite bank, and raises his head and roars his defiance at the world.

He is a lonesome bachelor. It is five or six years since he had a mate. She was shot by trophy-hunters, and the cubs, two of them, were trapped by men who trade in wild animals: one went to a circus, where it had to learn undignified tricks and respond to the flick of a whip, the other, more fortunate, went first to a zoo in Delhi and was later transferred to a zoo in America.

Sometimes, when the old tiger is very lonely, he gives a great roar, which can be heard throughout the forest. The villagers think he is roaring in anger, but the animals know that he is really roaring out of loneliness. When the sound of his roar has died away, he pauses, standing still, waiting for an answering roar, but it never comes. It is taken up instead by the shrill scream of a barbet high up in a sal tree.

It is dawn now, dew-fresh and cool, and the jungle dwellers are on the move. The black, beady little eyes of a jungle rat were fixed on a small brown hen who was returning cautiously to her nest. He had a large family to feed, and he knew that in the hen's nest was a clutch of delicious fawn-coloured eggs. He waited patiently for nearly an hour before he had the satisfaction of seeing the hen leave her nest and go off in search of food.

As soon as she had gone, the rat lost no time in making his raid. Slipping quietly out of his hole, he slithered along among the leaves, but, clever as he was, he did not realize that his own movements were being watched.

A pair of grey mongooses were scouting about in the dry grass. They, too, were hungry, and eggs usually figured large on their menu. Now, lying still on an outcrop of rock, they watched the rat sneaking along, occasionally sniffing at the air, and finally vanishing behind a boulder. When he reappeared, he was struggling to roll an egg uphill towards his hole.

The rat was in difficulties, pushing the egg sometimes with his paws, sometimes with his nose. The ground was rough, and the egg wouldn't go straight. Deciding that he must have help, he scuttled off to call his spouse. Even now the mongoose did not descend on that tantalizing egg. He waited until the rat returned with his wife, and then watched as the male rat took the egg firmly between his forepaws and rolled over on to his back. The female rat then grabbed her mate's tail and began to drag him along.

Totally absorbed in their struggle with the egg, the rats did not hear the approach of the mongooses. When these two large furry visitors suddenly bobbed up from behind a stone, the rats squealed with fright, abandoned the egg, and fled for their lives.

The mongooses wasted no time in breaking open the egg and making a meal of it. But just as, a few minutes ago, the rat had not noticed their approach, so now they did not notice the village boy, carrying a small bright axe and a net bag in his hands, creeping along.

Ramu too was searching for eggs, and when he saw the mongooses busy with one, he stood still to watch them, his eyes roving in search of the nest. He was hoping the mongooses would lead him to the nest, but, when they had finished their meal, the breeze took them in another direction, and Ramu had to do his own searching. He failed to find the nest, and moved further into the forest. The rat's hopes were just reviving when, to his disgust, the mother hen returned.

Ramu now made his way to a mahua tree.

The flowers of the mahua tree can be eaten by animals as well as men. Bears are particularly fond of them and will eat large quantities of its flowers which gradually start fermenting in their stomachs with the result that the animals get quite drunk. Ramu had often seen a couple of bears stumbling home to their cave, bumping into each other or into the trunks of trees—they are short-sighted to begin with, and when drunk can hardly see at all—but their sense of smell and hearing are so good that they finally find their way home.

Ramu decided he would gather some mahua flowers, and climbed swiftly into the tree, which is leafless when it blossoms. He began breaking the white flowers and throwing them to the ground. He had been in the tree for about five minutes when he heard the whining grumble of a bear, and presently a young sloth bear ambled into the clearing beneath the tree.

He was a small bear, little more than a cub, and Ramu was not frightened, but, because he thought the mother might be in the vicinity, he decided to take no chances, and sat very still, waiting to see what the bear would do. He hoped it wouldn't choose the same mahua tree for a meal.

At first the young bear put his nose to the ground and sniffed his way along until he came to a large white anthill. Here he began huffing and puffing, blowing rapidly in and out of his nostrils, so that the dust from the anthill flew in all directions. But he was a disappointed bear, because the anthill had been deserted long ago. And so, grumbling, he made his way across to a wild plum—a tall tree, the wild plum—and shinning rapidly up the smooth trunk, was soon perched in its topmost branches. It was only then that he saw Ramu.

The bear at once scrambled several feet higher up the tree, and laid himself out flat on a branch. It wasn't a very thick branch and left a large expanse of bear showing on either side of it. The bear tucked his head away behind another branch, and, so long as he could not see Ramu, seemed quite satisfied that he was well hidden, though he couldn't help grumbling with anxiety, for a bear, like most animals, is afraid of man—until he discovers that man is afraid of him.

Bears, however, are also very curious—and curiosity has often led them into trouble. Slowly, inch by inch, the young bear's black snout appeared over the edge of the branch, but, immediately, the eyes came into view and met Ramu's. He drew back with a jerk and the head was once more hidden. The bear did this two or three times, and Ramu, highly amused, waited until it wasn't looking, then moved some way down the tree. When the bear looked up again and saw that the boy was missing, he was so pleased with himself that he stretched right across to the next branch, to get at a plum. Ramu chose this moment to burst into loud laughter. The startled bear tumbled out of the tree, dropped through the branches for a distance of some fifteen feet, and landed with a thud in a heap of dry leaves.

And then several things happened almost at the same time.

The mother bear came charging into the clearing. Spotting Ramu in the tree, she reared up on her hind legs, grunting fiercely. It was Ramu's turn to be startled. There are few animals as dangerous as a rampaging mother bear, and the boy knew that one blow from her clawed forepaws could rip his skull open.

But before the bear could approach the tree, there was a tremendous roar, and the tiger bounded into the clearing. He had been asleep in the bushes not far away—he liked a good sleep after a heavy meal—and the noise in the clearing had woken him.

He was in a very bad temper, and his loud 'A—oonh!' made his displeasure quite clear. The bears turned and ran from the clearing, the youngster squealing with fright.

The tiger then came into the centre of the clearing, looked up at the trembling boy, and roared again.

Ramu nearly fell out of the tree.

'Good day to you, Uncle,' he stammered, showing his teeth in a nervous grin.

Perhaps this was too much for the tiger. With a low growl, he turned his back on the mahua tree and padded off into the jungle, his tail twitching in disgust.

※

That night, when Ramu told his parents and grandfather about the tiger and how it had saved him from a female bear, a number of stories were told about tigers, some of whom had been gentlemen, others rogues. Sooner or later the conversation came round to man-eaters, and Grandfather told two stories, which he swore were true, though the others only half believed him.

The first story concerned the belief that a man-eating tiger is guided towards his next victim by the spirit of a human being previously killed and eaten by the tiger. Grandfather said that he actually knew three hunters who sat up in a machan over a human kill, and when the tiger came, the corpse sat up and pointed with his right hand at the men in the tree. The tiger then went away. But the hunters knew he would return, and one man was brave enough to get down from the tree and tie the right arm of the corpse to the body. Later, when the tiger returned, the corpse sat up and pointed out the men with his left hand. The enraged tiger sprang into the tree and killed his enemies in the machan.

'And then there was a bania,' said Grandfather, beginning another story, 'who lived in a village in the jungle. He wanted to visit a neighbouring village to collect some money that was owed him, but as the road lay through heavy forest, in which lived a terrible man-eating tiger, he did not know what to do. Finally, he went to a sadhu who gave him two powders. By eating the first powder, he could turn into a huge tiger, capable of dealing with any other tiger in the jungle, and by eating the second he could become a bania again.

'Armed with his two powders, and accompanied by his pretty young wife, the bania set out on his journey. They had not gone far into the forest when they came upon the man-eater sitting in the middle of the road. Before swallowing the first powder, the bania told his wife to stay where she was, so that when he returned after killing the tiger, she could at once give him the second powder and enable him to resume his old shape.

'Well, the bania's plan worked, but only up to a point. He swallowed the first powder and immediately became a magnificent tiger. With a great roar, he bounded towards the man-eater, and after a brief, furious fight, killed his opponent. Then, with his jaws still dripping blood, he returned to his wife.

'The poor girl was terrified and spilt the second powder on the ground. The bania was so angry that he pounced on his wife and killed and ate her. And afterwards this terrible tiger was so enraged at not being able to become a human again that he killed and ate hundreds of people all over the country.'

'The only people he spared,' said Grandfather, with a twinkle in his eye, 'were those who owed him money. A bania never gives up a loan as lost, and the tiger still hoped that one day he might become a human again and be able to collect his dues.'

Next morning, when Ramu came back from the well which was used to irrigate his father's fields, he found a crowd of curious children surrounding a jeep and three strangers with guns. Each of the strangers had a gun, and they were accompanied by two bearers and a vast amount of provisions.

They had heard that there was a tiger in the area, and they wanted to shoot it.

One of the hunters, who looked even stranger than the others, had come all the way to India for tiger, and he had vowed that he would not leave the country without a tiger's skin in his baggage. One of his companions had said that he could buy a tiger's skin in Delhi, but the hunter did not like the idea and said he'd have nothing to do with a tiger that he hadn't shot.

These men had money to spend, and, as most of the villagers needed money badly, they were only too willing to construct a machan for the hunters. The platform, big enough to take the three men, was put up in the branches of a tall toon, or mahogany tree.

It was the only night the hunters used the machan. At the end of March, though the days are warm, the nights are still cold. The hunters had neglected to bring blankets, and by midnight their teeth were chattering. Ramu, having tied up a goat for them at the foot of the tree, made as if to go home but instead circled the area, hanging up bits and pieces of old clothing on small trees and bushes. He thought he owed that much to the tiger. He knew the wily old king of the jungle would keep well away from the goat if he thought there were humans in the vicinity. And where there are men's clothes, there will be men.

As soon as it was dark, the goat began bleating, loud enough for any self-respecting tiger to hear it, but perhaps the ruse was too obvious, or perhaps the clothes Ramu had hung out were warning enough, because the tiger did not come near the toon tree. In any case, the men in the tree soon gave themselves away.

The cold was really too much for them. A flask of brandy was produced, and passed round, and it was not long before there was more purpose to finishing the brandy than to finishing off a tiger. Silent at first, the men soon began talking in whispers, and to jungle creatures a human whisper is as telling as a trumpet call. Soon the men were quite merry, talking in loud voices. And when the first morning light crept over the forest, and Ramu and his friends came by to see if the goat still lived, they found the hunters fast asleep in the machan.

The shikaris looked surly and embarrassed when they trudged back to the village.

'No game left in these parts,' said one.

'The wrong time of the year for tiger,' said another.

'I don't know what the country's coming to,' said the third.

And complaining about the weather, the quality of cartridges, the quality of rum, and the perversity of tigers, they drove away in disgust.

It was not until the onset of summer that an event occurred which altered the hunting habits of the tiger and brought him into conflict with the villagers.

※

There had been no rain for almost two months, and the grass had become a dry yellow. Some refugee settlers, living in an area where the forest had been cleared, were careless in putting out a fire. The tiger sniffed at the acrid smell of smoke in the air, and, wandering to the edge of the jungle, saw in the distance the dancing lights of a forest fire. As night came on, the flames grew more vivid, the smell stronger. The tiger turned and made for the jheel, where he knew he would be safe, provided he swam across to the little island in the centre.

Next morning he was on the island, which was untouched by the fire. But his surroundings had changed. The slopes of the hills were black with burnt grass, and most of the tall bamboo had disappeared. The deer and the wild pig, finding that their natural cover had gone, fled further east.

The tiger prowled throughout the smoking forest but he found no game. Once he came across the body of a burnt rabbit, but he could not eat it. He drank at the jheel and settled down in a shady spot to sleep the day away. Perhaps, by evening, some of the animals would return. If not, he too would have to look for new hunting grounds—or new game.

The tiger had not eaten for five days and he was so hungry that he had been forced to scratch about in the grass and leaves for worms and beetles. This was a sad comedown for the king of the jungle. But even now he hesitated to leave the area, for he had a deep suspicion and fear of the forests further south and east—forests that were fast being swallowed up by human habitation. He could have gone north, into the hills, but they did not provide him with the long grass he needed. A panther could manage quite well in the hills, but not a tiger who loved the natural privacy of heavy jungle. In the hills, he would have to hide all the time.

At break of day, the tiger came to the jheel. The water was now shallow and muddy, and a green scum had spread over the top. But the water was still drinkable, and the tiger had quenched his thirst.

He lay down across his favourite rock, hoping for a deer, but none approached. He was about to get up and go away when he heard the warning chatter of a lone langur. Some animal was definitely approaching.

The tiger at once dropped flat on the ground, his tawny skin merging with the dry grass. A heavy animal was moving through the bushes, and the tiger waited patiently until a buffalo emerged and came to the water. The buffalo was alone.

He was a big male buffalo, and his long curved horns lay right back across his shoulders. He moved leisurely towards the water, completely unaware of the tiger's presence.

The tiger hesitated before making his charge. It was a long time—many years—since he had killed a buffalo, and he knew the villagers would not like it. But hunger helped him to overcome his caution. There was no morning breeze, everything was still, and the smell of the tiger did not carry to the buffalo. The monkey still chattered in a nearby tree, but his warning went unheeded.

Moving at a crouch, the tiger skirted the edge of the jheel and approached the buffalo from the rear. The water birds, who were used to the presence of both animals, did not raise an alarm.

Getting closer, the tiger glanced around to see if there were men, or other buffaloes, in the vicinity. Then, satisfied that he was alone, he crept forward. The buffalo was drinking, standing in shallow water at the edge of the tank, when the tiger charged from the side and bit deep into the animal's thigh.

The buffalo turned to fight, but the tendons of his right hind leg had been snapped, and he could only stagger forward a few paces. But he was not afraid. He bellowed, and lowered his horns at the tiger, but the great cat was too fast and, circling the buffalo, bit into the other hind leg.

The buffalo crashed to the ground, both hind legs crippled, and then the tiger dashed in, using both tooth and claw, biting deep into the buffalo's throat until the blood gushed out from the jugular vein.

The buffalo gave one long last bellow before dying.

The tiger, having rested, now began to gorge himself, but,

even though he had been starving for days, he could not finish the buffalo. At least one good meal still remained when, satisfied and feeling his strength return, he quenched his thirst at the jheel. Then he dragged the remains of the buffalo into the bushes and went off to find a place to sleep. He would return to the kill when he was hungry.

The villagers were upset when they discovered that a buffalo was missing, and next day, when Ramu and Shyam came running home to say that they had found the carcass near the jheel, half-eaten by the tiger, the men were disturbed and angry. They felt that the tiger had tricked and deceived them. And they knew that once he found he could kill buffaloes quite easily, he would make a habit of it.

Kundan Singh, Shyam's father, and the owner of the dead buffalo, said he would go after the tiger himself.

'It is all very well to talk about what you will do to the tiger,' said his wife, 'but you should never have let the buffalo go off on its own.'

'He had been out on his own before,' said Kundan. 'This is the first time the tiger has attacked one of our beasts. A shaitan—a devil—has entered the Maharaj.'

'He must have been very hungry,' said Shyam.

'Well, we are hungry too,' said Kundan. 'Our best buffalo—the only male in our herd—'

'The tiger will kill again,' said Ramu's father.

'If we let him,' said Kundan. 'Should we send for the shikaris?'

'No. They were not clever. The tiger will escape them easily. And, besides, there is no time. The tiger will return for another meal tonight. We must finish him off ourselves!'

'But how?'

Kundan Singh smiled secretively, played with the ends of his moustache for a few moments, and then, with great pride, produced from under his cot a double-barrelled gun of ancient vintage.

'My father bought it from an Englishman,' he said.

'How long ago was that?'

'At the time I was born.'

'And have you ever used it?' asked Ramu's father, who was not sure that the gun would work.

'Well, some years back, I let it off at some bandits. You remember the time when those dacoits raided our village? They chose the wrong village, and were severely beaten for their pains. As they left, I fired my gun off at them, and as a result they didn't stop running until they had crossed the Ganga!'

'Yes, but did you hit anyone?'

'I would have, if someone's goat hadn't got in the way at the last moment. But we had roast mutton that night! Don't worry, brother, I know how the thing works. It takes a fistful of powder and bullets the size of pigeon's eggs!'

Accompanied by Ramu's father and some others, Kundan set out for the jheel, where, without shifting the buffalo's carcass—for they knew the tiger would not come near them if it suspected a trap—they made another machan in a tall tree some thirty feet from the kill.

Later that evening—at the 'hour of cow-dust', Kundan Singh and Ramu's father settled down for the night on their crude tree platform.

Several hours passed, and nothing but a jackal was seen by the watchers. And then, just as the moon came up over the distant hills, Kundan and his companion were startled by a low 'A—oonh', followed by a suppressed, rumbling growl.

Kundan grasped his old gun, while his friend drew closer to him for comfort. There was complete silence for a minute or two—a time that was an agony of suspense for the watchers—and then there was the sound of a stealthy footfall on some dead leaves under the tree.

A moment later the tiger walked out into the moonlight and stood over his kill.

At first Kundan could do nothing. He was completely overawed by the size of this magnificent tiger. Ramu's father had to nudge him, and then Kundan quickly put the gun to his shoulder, aimed at the tiger's head, and pressed the trigger.

The gun went off with a flash and a tremendous roar, but the bullet only singed the tiger's shoulder.

The enraged animal rushed at the tree and tried to leap into its branches. Fortunately the machan had been built at a safe height, and the tiger, unable to reach it, roared twice, and then bounded off into the forest.

'What a tiger!' exclaimed Kundan, half in fear and half in admiration. 'I feel as though my liver has turned to water.'

'You missed him completely,' said Ramu's father. 'Your gun makes a big noise, but an arrow would have been more accurate.'

'I did not miss him,' said Kundan, feeling offended. 'You heard him roar, didn't you? He would not have been so angry if he had not been hit. If I have wounded him badly, he will die.'

'And if you have wounded him slightly, he may turn into a man-eater, and then where will we be?'

'I don't think he will come back,' said Kundan. 'He will leave these forests.'

They waited until the sun was up before coming down from the tree. They found a few drops of blood on the dry grass, but no trail led into the forest, and Ramu's father was convinced that the wound was only a slight one.

The bullet, missing the fatal spot behind the ear, had only grazed the back of the skull and cut a deep groove at its base.

It took a few days to heal, and during this time the tiger lay low and did not go near the jheel except when it was very dark and he was very thirsty. The villagers thought the tiger had gone away, and Ramu and Shyam—accompanied by some other youths, and always carrying sticks and axes—began bringing the buffaloes to the tank again during the day; but they were careful not to let any of them stray far from the herd, and they returned home while it was still daylight.

While the buffaloes wallowed in the muddy water, and the boys wrestled on their grassy islet, a tawny eagle circled high above them, looking for a meal—a sure sign that some of the animals were beginning to return to the forest. It was not long before his keen eyes detected a movement in the glade below.

What the eagle saw was a baby hare, a small fluffy thing, its long pink-tinted ears laid flat along its sides. Had it not been creeping along between two large stones, it would have escaped notice. The eagle waited to see if the mother was about, and even as he waited he realized that he was not the only one who coveted this juicy hare. From the bushes there had appeared a sinuous yellow creature, pressed low to the ground and moving rapidly towards the hare. It was a yellow jungle cat, hardly noticeable in the scorched grass. With great stealth and artistry the jungle cat stalked the baby hare.

He pounced. The hare's squeal was cut short by the cat's cruel claws, but it had been heard by the mother hare, who now bounded into the glade and without the slightest hesitation attacked the surprised cat.

There was nothing haphazard about the hare's attack. She flashed around behind the cat and jumped clean over it. As she landed, she kicked back, sending a stinging jet of dust shooting into the cat's face. She did this again and again.

The bewildered cat, crouching and snarling, picked up the kill and tried to run away with it. But the hare would not permit this. She continued her leaping and buffeting till eventually the cat, out of sheer frustration, dropped the kill and attacked the mother.

The cat sprang at the hare a score of times lashing out with its claws, but the mother hare was both clever and agile enough to keep just out of reach of those terrible claws, and drew the cat further and further away from her baby—for she did not as yet know that it was dead.

The tawny eagle saw his chance. Swift and true, he swooped.

For a brief moment, as his wings overspread the furry little hare and his talons sank deep into it, he caught a glimpse of the cat racing towards him and the mother hare fleeing into the bushes. And then, with a shrill 'kee-ee-ee' of triumph, he rose and whirled away with his dinner.

The boys had heard this shrill cry and looked up just in time to see the eagle flying over the jheel with the small hare held firmly in its talons.

'Poor hare,' said Shyam. 'Its life was short.'

'That's the law of the jungle,' said Ramu. 'The eagle has a family too, and must feed it.'

'I wonder if we are any better than animals,' said Shyam.

'Perhaps we are a little better,' said Ramu. 'Grandfather always says, "To be able to laugh and to be merciful are the only things that make man better than the beast".'

❦

The next day, while the boys were taking the herd home, one of the buffaloes lagged behind. Ramu did not know the animal was missing until he heard her agonized bellow. He glanced over his shoulder just in time to see the big striped tiger dragging the buffalo into a clump of young bamboo. At the same time the herd became aware of the danger, and the buffaloes snorted with fear as they hurried along the forest path. To urge them forward, and to warn his friends, Ramu cupped his hands to his mouth and gave vent to a yodelling call.

The buffaloes bellowed, the boys shouted, and the birds flew shrieking from the trees. It was almost a stampede by the time the herd emerged from the forest. The villagers heard the thunder of hoofs, and saw the herd coming home in dust and confusion, and knew that something was wrong. 'The tiger!' shouted Ramu. 'He is here! He has killed one of the buffaloes.'

'He is afraid of us no longer,' said Shyam.

'Did you see where he went?' asked Kundan Singh, hurrying

up to them.

'I remember the place,' said Ramu. 'He dragged the buffalo in amongst the bamboo.'

'Then there is no time to lose,' said his father.

'Kundan, you take your gun and two men, and wait near the suspension bridge, where the Garur stream joins the Ganga. The jungle narrows there. We will beat the jungle from our side, and drive the tiger towards you. He will not escape us, unless he swims the river!'

'Good!' said Kundan, running into his house for his gun, with Shyam close at his heels. 'Was it one of our buffaloes again?' he asked.

'It was Ramu's buffalo this time,' said Shyam, 'A good milk buffalo.'

'Then Ramu's father will beat the jungle thoroughly. You boys had better come with me. It will not be safe for you to accompany the beaters.'

※

And so, Kundan Singh carrying his gun and accompanied by Ramu, Shyam and two men, headed for the river junction, while Ramu's father collected about twenty men from the village and, guided by one of the boys who had been with Ramu, made for the spot where the tiger had killed the buffalo.

The tiger was still eating when he heard the men coming. He had not expected to be disturbed so soon. With an angry 'Whoof!' he bounded into the bamboo thicket and watched the men through a screen of leaves and tall grass.

The men did not seem to take much notice of the dead buffalo, but gathered round their leader and held a consultation. Most of them carried hand drums which hung down to their waists by shoulder-straps. They also carried sticks, spears and axes.

After a hurried conversation, they turned to face the jungle and began beating their drums with the palms of their hands.

Some of the men banged empty kerosene tins. These made even more noise than the drums.

The tiger did not like the noise and retreated further into the jungle. But he was surprised to find that the men, instead of going away, came after him into the jungle, banging away on their drums and tins, and shouting at the top of their voices. They had separated now, and advanced singly or in pairs, but nowhere were they more than fifteen yards apart. The tiger could easily have broken through this slowly advancing semicircle of men—one swift blow from his paw would have felled the strongest of them—but his main aim was to get away from the noise. He hated and feared the noise made by men.

He was not a man-eater and he would not attack a man unless he was very angry or very frightened or very desperate; and he was none of these things as yet. He had eaten well, and he would like to rest in peace—but there would be no rest for any animal until the men had gone with their tremendous clatter and din.

For an hour Ramu's father and the others beat the jungle, calling, drumming and trampling the undergrowth. The tiger had no rest. Whenever he was able to put some distance between himself and the men, he would sink down in some shady spot to rest, but, within five or ten minutes, the trampling and drumming would sound nearer, and the tiger, with an angry snarl, would get up and pad silently north along the narrowing strip of jungle, towards the junction of the Garur stream and the Ganga. Ten years back, he would have had jungle on his right in which to hide; but the trees had been felled long ago, to make way for more humans, and now he could only move to the left, towards the river.

It was about noon when the tiger finally appeared in the open. He longed for the darkness and security of the night, for the sun was his enemy. Kundan and the boys had a clear view of him as he stalked slowly along, now in the open with the sun glinting on his glossy side, now in the shade, or passing through the shorter reeds. He was still out of range of Kundan's gun, but there was no fear of his getting out of the beat, as the 'stops' were all picked men from the village. He disappeared among some bushes but soon reappeared to retrace his steps, the beaters having done their work well. He was now only one hundred and fifty yards from the rocks where Kundan Singh waited, and he looked very big.

※

The beat had closed in, and his exit along the bank downstream was completely blocked; so the tiger turned into a belt of reeds, and Kundan Singh expected that his head would soon peer out of the cover a few yards away. The beaters were now making a great noise, shouting and beating their drums, but nothing moved, and Ramu, watching from a distance, wondered, 'Has he slipped through the beaters?' And hoped he had.

Tins clashed, drums beat, and some of the men poked into the reeds with their spears or long bamboos. Perhaps one of these thrusts found a mark, because at last the tiger was roused, and with an angry, desperate snarl he charged out of the reeds, splashing his way through an inlet of mud and water.

Kundan Singh fired, and his bullet struck the tiger on the thigh.

The mighty animal stumbled; but he was up in a minute, and, rushing through a gap in the narrowing line of beaters, he made straight for the only way across the river—the suspension bridge that passed over the Ganga here, providing a route into the high hills beyond.

'We'll get him now,' said Kundan, priming his gun again. 'He's right in the open!'

The suspension bridge swayed and trembled as the wounded tiger lurched across it. Kundan fired, and this time the bullet hit the tiger on the shoulder. The animal bounded forward, lost his footing on the unfamiliar, slippery planks of the swaying bridge, and went over the side, falling headlong into the strong, swirling waters of the river.

He rose to the surface once, but the current took him under and away, and only a thin streak of blood remained on the river's surface.

Kundan and the others hurried downstream to see if the dead tiger had been washed up on the river's banks; but though they searched the riverside for several miles, they did not find the tiger. The river had taken him to its bosom. He had not provided anyone with a trophy. His skin would not be spread on a couch, nor would his head be hung upon a wall. No claw of his would be hung as a charm around the neck of a child. No villager would use his fat as a cure for rheumatism.

At first the villagers were glad because they felt their buffaloes were safe. Then the men began to feel that something had gone out of their lives, out of the life of the forest; they began to feel that the forest was no longer a forest. It had been shrinking year after year, but, as long as the tiger had been there and the villagers had heard it roar at night, they had known that they were still secure from the intruders and newcomers who came to fell the trees and eat up the land and let the floodwaters into the village. But, now that the tiger had gone, it was as though a protector had gone, leaving the forest open and vulnerable, easily destroyable. And, once the forest was destroyed, they too would be in danger...

There was another thing that had gone with the tiger, another thing that had been lost, a thing that was being lost everywhere—something called 'nobility'.

Ramu remembered something that his grandfather had once said, 'The tiger is the very soul of India, and when the last tiger has gone, so will the soul of the country.'

The boys lay flat on their stomachs on their little mud island and watched the monsoon clouds gathering overhead.

'The king of our forest is dead,' said Shyam. 'There are no more tigers.'

'There must be tigers,' said Ramu. 'How can there be an India without tigers?'

The river had carried the tiger many miles away from its home, from the forest it had always known, and brought it ashore on a strip of warm yellow sand, where it lay in the sun, quite still but breathing.

Vultures gathered and waited at a distance, some of them perching on the branches of nearby trees.

But the tiger was more drowned than hurt, and as the river water oozed out of his mouth, and the warm sun made new life throb through his body, he stirred and stretched, and his glazed eyes came into focus. Raising his head, he saw trees and tall grass.

Slowly he heaved himself off the ground and moved at a crouch to where the grass waved in the afternoon breeze. Would he be harried again, and shot at? There was no smell of Man. The tiger moved forward with greater confidence.

There was, however, another smell in the air—a smell that reached back to the time when he was young and fresh and full of vigour—a smell that he had almost forgotten but could never quite forget—the smell of a tigress!

He raised his head high, and new life surged through his tired limbs. He gave a full-throated roar and moved purposefully through the tall grass. And the roar came back to him, calling him, calling him forward—a roar that meant there would be more tigers in the land.

TIGER IN THE CEMETERY

Lady Wart of Worcester, Lady Tryiton and the Earl of Stopwater, the Hon'ble Robin Crazier, Mr and Mrs Paddy Snott-Noble, the Earl and Countess of Lost Marbles and General Sir Peter de l'Orange-Peel...

These were only some of the gracious names that graced the pages of the Doon Club's guest and membership register at the turn of the century, when the town was the favourite retiring place for English aristocracy. So well did the club look after its members that most of them remained permanently in Dehra, to be buried in the Chandernagar cemetery just off the Haridwar Road.

My own ancestors were not aristocracy. Dad's father came to India as an eighteen-year-old soldier in a Scots regiment, a contemporary of Kipling's 'Soldiers Three'—Privates Othenis, Mulvaney and Learoyd. He married an orphaned girl who had been brought up on an indigo plantation at Motihari in Bihar. My maternal grandfather worked in the Indian Railways, as a foreman in the railway workshops at some godforsaken railway junction in central India. He married a statuesque, strong-willed lady who had also grown up in India. Dad was born in the Shahjahanpur military camp; my mother in Karachi. So although my forebears were, for the most part, European, I was third generation India-born. The expression 'Anglo-Indian' has come to mean so many things—British settler, Old Koi-Hai, Colonel Curry or Captain Chapatti, or simply Eurasian—that I don't use it very often. Indian is good enough for me. I may have relatives scattered around the world, but I have no great interest in meeting them. My feet are firmly planted in the Ganga soil.

Grandfather (of the Railways) retired in Dehradun (or Deyrah Dhoon, as it was spelt in the old days) and built a sturdy bungalow on the Old Survey Road. Sadly, it was sold at the time of Independence when most of his children decided to quit the country. After my father's death, my mother married a Punjabi gentleman and so I stayed on in India, except for that brief sojourn in England and the Channel Islands. I'd come back to Dehra to find that even mother and stepfather had left, but it was still home, and in the cemetery there were several relatives including Grandfather and Great-grandmother. If I sat on their graves, I felt I owned a bit of property. Not a bungalow or even a vegetable patch, but a few feet of well-nourished sod. There were even marigolds flowering at the edge of the graves. And a little blue everlasting that I have always associated with Dehra. It grows in ditches, on vacant plots, in neglected gardens, along footpaths, on the edges of fields, behind lime-kilns, wherever there is a bit of wasteland. Call it a weed if you like, but I have every respect for a plant that will survive the onslaught of brick, cement, petrol fumes, grazing cows and goats, heat and cold (for it flowers almost all the year round) and overflowing sewage. As long as that little flowering weed is still around, there is hope for both man and nature.

A feeling of tranquillity and peace always pervaded my being when I entered the cemetery. Were my long-gone relatives pleased by my presence there? I did not see them in any form, but then, cemeteries are the last place for departed souls to hang around in. Given a chance, they would rather be among the living, near those they cared for or in places where they were happy. I have never been convinced by ghost stories in which the tormented spirit revisits the scene of some ghastly tragedy. Why on earth (or why in heaven) should they want to relive an unpleasant experience?

My maternal grandfather, by my mother's account, was a man with a sly sense of humour who often discomfited his relatives by introducing into their homes odd creatures who refused to go away. Hence, the tiny Jharipani bat released in Aunt Mabel's bedroom, or the hedgehog slipped between his brother Major Clerke's bedsheets. A cousin, Mrs Blanchette, found her house swarming with white rats, while a neighbour received a gift of a parcel of papayas—and in their midst, a bright green - and - yellow chameleon.

And so, when I was within some fifty to sixty feet of Grandfather's grave, I was not in the least surprised to see a full-grown tiger stretched out on his tombstone, apparently enjoying the shade of the magnolia tree which grew beside it.

Was this a manifestation of the tiger cub he'd kept when I was a child? Did the ghosts of long-dead tigers enjoy visiting old haunts? Live tigers certainly did, and when this one stirred, yawned and twitched its tail, I decided I wouldn't stay to find out if it was a phantom tiger or a real one.

Beating a hasty retreat to the watchman's quarters near the lychgate, I noticed a large, well-fed and very real goat tethered to one of the old tombstones (Colonel Ponsonby of Her Majesty's Dragoons), and I concluded that the tiger had already spotted it and was simply building up an appetite before lunch.

'There's a tiger on Grandfather's grave,' I called out to the watchman, who was checking out his cabbage patch. (And healthy cabbages they were, too.)

The watchman was a bit deaf and assumed that I was complaining about some member of his family, as they were in the habit of grinding their masalas on the smoother gravestones.

'It's that boy Masood,' he said. 'I'll get after him with a stick.' And picking up his lathi, he made for the grave.

A yell, a roar and the watchman was back and out of the lychgate before me.

'Send for the police, sahib,' he shouted. 'It's one of the circus tigers. It must have escaped!'

Sincerely hoping that Sitaram (a friend of mine who had managed to land a job at the circus) had not been in the way of the escaping tiger, I made for the circus tents on the parade ground. There was no show in progress. It was about noon, and everyone appeared to be resting. If a tiger was missing, no one seemed to be aware of it.

'Where's Sitaram?' I asked one of the hands.

'Helping to wash down the ponies,' he replied.

But he wasn't in the pony enclosure. So I made my way to the rear, where there was a cage housing a lion (looking rather sleepy, after its late-night bout with the lady lion tamer), another cage housing a tiger (looking ready to bite my head off) and another cage with its door open—empty!

Someone came up behind me, whistling cheerfully. It was Sitaram.

'Do you like the tigers?' he asked.

'There's only one here. There are three in the show, aren't there?'

'Of course, I helped feed them this morning.'

'Well, one of them's gone for a walk. Someone must have unlocked the door. If it's the same tiger I saw in the cemetery, I think it's looking for another meal—or maybe just dessert!'

Sitaram ran back into the tent, yelling for the trainer and the ringmaster. And then, of course, there was commotion. For no one had noticed the tiger slipping away. It must have made off through the bamboo-grove at the edge of the parade ground, through the Forest Rangers College (well-wooded then), circled the police lines and entered the cemetery. By now it could have been anywhere.

It was, in fact, walking right down the middle of Dehra's main road, causing the first hold-up in traffic since Pandit Nehru's last visit to the town. Mr Nehru would have fancied the notion; he was keen on tigers. But the citizens of Dehra took no chances.

They scattered at the noble beast's approach. The Delhi bus came to a grinding halt, while tonga-ponies, never known to move faster than a brisk trot, broke into a gallop that would have done them proud at the Bangalore Races.

The only creature that failed to move was a large bull (the one that sometimes blocked the approach to my steps) sitting in the middle of the road, forming a traffic island of its own. It did not move for cars, buses, tongas and trucks. Why budge for a mere tiger?

And the tiger, having been fed on butcher's meat most of his life, now disdained the living thing (since the bull refused to be stalked) and headed instead for the back entrance to the Indiana's kitchens.

There was a general exodus from the Indiana. William Matheson, who had been regaling his friends with tales of his exploits in the Foreign Legion, did not hang around either; he made for the comparative safety of my flat. Larry Gomes stopped in the middle of playing the *Anniversary Waltz,* and foxtrotted out of the restaurant. The owner of the Indiana rushed into the street and collided with the owner of the Royal Café. Both swore at each other in choice Pashtu—they were originally from Peshawar. Swami Aiyar, a Doon School boy with ambitions of being a newspaper correspondent, buttonholed me near my landlady's shop and asked me if I knew Jim Corbett's telephone number in Haldwani.

'But he only shoots man-eaters,' I protested.

'Well, they're saying three people have already been eaten in the bazaar.'

'Ridiculous. No self-respecting tiger would go for a three-course meal.'

'All the same, people are in danger.'

'So, we'll send for Jim Corbett. Aurora of the Green Bookshop should have his number.'

Mr Aurora was better informed than either of us. He told

us that Jim Corbett had settled in Kenya several years ago.

Swami looked dismayed. 'I thought he loved India so much that he refused to leave.'

'You're confusing him with Jack Gibson of the Mayo School,' I said.

At this point the tiger came through the swing doors of the Indiana and started crossing the road. Suresh Mathur was driving slowly down Rajpur Road in his 1936 Hillman. He'd been up half the night, drinking and playing cards, and he had a terrible hangover. He was now heading for the Royal Café, convinced that only a chilled beer could help him recover. When he saw the tiger, his reflexes—never very good—failed him completely, and he drove his car onto the pavement and into the plate-glass window of Bhai Dhian Singh's Wine and Liquor Shop. Suresh looked quite happy among the broken rum bottles. The heady aroma of XXX Rosa rum, awash on the shopping veranda, was too much for a couple of old topers, who began to mop up the liquor with their handkerchiefs. Suresh would have done the same had he been conscious.

We carried him to the deserted Indiana and sent for Dr Sharma.

'Nothing much wrong with him,' said the doctor, 'but he looks anaemic,' and he proceeded to give him an injection of vitamin B12. This was Dr Sharma's favourite remedy for anyone who was ailing. He was a great believer in vitamins.

I don't know if the B12 did Suresh any good, but the jab of the needle woke him up, and he looked around, blinked up at me and said, 'Thought I saw a tiger. Could do with a drink, old boy.'

'I'll stand you a beer,' I said. 'But you'll have to pay the bill at Bhai Dhian's. And your car needs repairs.'

'And this injection costs five rupees,' said Dr Sharma.

'Beer is the same price. I'll stand you one too.'

So we settled down in the Indiana and finished several bottles of beer, Dr Sharma expounding all the time on the miracle of vitamin B12, while Suresh told me that he knew now what it felt like to enter the fourth dimension.

The tiger was soon forgotten, and when I walked back to my room a couple of hours later and found the postman waiting for me with a twenty-five rupee money order from *Sainik Samachar* (the Armed Forces' weekly magazine), I tipped him five rupees and put the rest aside for a rainy day—which, hopefully, would be the morrow, as monsoon clouds had been advancing from the south.

They say that those with a clear conscience usually sleep well. I have always done a lot of sleeping, especially in the afternoons, and have never been unduly disturbed by pangs of conscience, for I haven't deprived any man of his money, his wife or his song.

I kicked off my chappals and lay down and allowed my mind to dwell on my favourite Mexican proverb, 'How sweet it is to do nothing, and afterwards to rest!'

I hoped the tiger had found a shady spot for his afternoon siesta. With goodwill towards one and all, I drifted into a deep sleep and woke only in the early evening, to the sound of distant thunder.

MRS ROBERTS

Elsie Roberts had been quite a beauty in her twenties and thirties—one of those fair Anglo-Indians who passed for European until their accents gave them away. Elsie, it was said, did her best to remain fair, staying out of the sun as much as possible. In her later years, she was seldom seen during the day, but by then she had lost her looks and taken to drink; she slept by day and lived by night.

In her heyday Elsie (nee MacGowan) was a dancing partner to Roberts, a good-looking French Jew who had made his way to India just before World War II broke out. They danced in Cabaret at the Imperial and Swiss in Delhi, and at Hakman's in Mussoorie, and Filetto's in Lahore. They made an elegant pair—they danced beautifully. Inevitably, they were compared to Fred Astaire and Ginger Rogers, the dancing sensation of the silver screen. They married, and continued to partner each other until the war ended. Then, Roberts made a trip to France to claim and collect some compensation due to him as a war refugee. As he stood at the cashier's counter, waiting for the first instalment to be handed over to him, he collapsed and died of a heart attack. Chance gives, and takes away, and sometimes gives again, but human life is equally unpredictable.

However, Elsie, as his widow, was entitled to the proceeds. She gave up her dancing career and took to breeding dogs. I first saw her when she came to see my mother in New Delhi, sometime in 1958. My mother was breeding Poms, and Elsie bought a small black Pom. She was still very attractive (Elsie not the Pom) and was escorted by a gentleman who owned a small restaurant in Mussoorie.

'He's after the money,' said my mother later, and she was right, as the gentleman in question wheedled a large sum of money out of her and then deserted her.

Elsie transferred her affections to her dogs. She rented a house outside Mussoorie and provided board and lodging to a large variety of canines. There was considerable inbreeding. Poms wed dachshunds, Samoyeds wed spaniels, and Labradors wed German shepherds. The resultant mixture was undistinguished, to say the least. Elsie didn't care. She had become devoted to her dogs and had no desire to sell them, with or without pedigree. She fed them well, and the local butcher proclaimed that she was his best customer.

Of course, strays and village dogs also found their way on to the premises. When there are free lunches to be had, dogs and humans are no different. Word soon gets around and everyone drops in for the wedding feast.

They were not a ferocious lot. Like their owner, they were wary of humans, quite paranoid about them. They'd bark furiously but scatter at the approach of anything on two legs.

When I came to live in Mussoorie in the mid-1960s, I thought I'd pay a casual visit to Mrs Roberts; my mother had asked me to look her up. She was then living near Barlowganj, where she had a huge bungalow to herself, most of it occupied by some twenty to thirty dogs.

At first she refused to see me, but when I told her who I was, she let me in. 'So you're Edie's son,' she said. 'How is your mother?'

'Not too well, I'm afraid.'

'Does she still have her Poms?'

'Several of them.' I refrained from adding that they were a bloody nuisance. Try sharing a Delhi flat with half-a-dozen snapping, yapping, highly strung, hysterical Poms—my least favourite breed!

Mrs Roberts showed me around. The house was filthy. She was equally unkempt—her dress soiled, hands and feet unwashed, hair all over the place. Only traces of her former beauty remained. She was in her late forties, and fading fast.

But she was to live another twenty years.

The next time I saw her, about five years later, she was in considerable distress. Two or three of her dogs were suffering from mange and had to be put down. But the vet's injections hadn't worked properly (it was probably some spurious stuff) and the dogs died slowly and painfully. Mrs Roberts went further into her shell, and moved with her companions to the top of the mountain, near Sister's bazaar. Old-timers in that area still remember her.

She would emerge from her house once a month, to collect her money from the local bank. The rest of the time she would remain locked up with her dogs, emerging only to receive the butcher, or the milkman who also brought her the local brew, a potent distillation made from mysterious ingredients. At the time we were going through a period of Prohibition (it was Morarji's government), but Mrs Roberts and the local villagers had beaten the system.

I, too, had come to rely on the local milkman as a source of supply. 'English wines and spirits' having been taken off the market, Kachi-sharab, the special from Kotti, Kanda and other gaons, was the only alternative. My milkman used my hot-water bottle to bring me the stuff. Unfortunately, the hot-water bottle stank for weeks afterwards, and could no longer be used for legitimate purposes. No matter. Those were desperate times.

Mrs Roberts had been on the stuff for years and was apparently none the worse for it. Prohibition came and went, and politicians came and went, and while frail creatures such as I returned to mere whisky and water, tougher souls, such as Elsie Roberts, continued with the local stuff, which was certainly more potent.

Two or three years passed, and I had forgotten Mrs Roberts and her dogs, when one morning the local missionary-doctor, Dr Olsen, dropped in to tell me she had died in the night (of double pneumonia) and did I know if she had any relatives.

'None that I know of,' I had to say, 'just those dogs.'

She was given a pauper's burial in the little burial ground below Woodstock, where some of the school's Christian servants were laid to rest. No tombstones there. As a beautiful young dancer she'd been the toast of Mussoorie. That had been over forty years ago. Now, friendless, she had been swept away like a dead leaf.

And what of the dogs?

Bereft of their benefactor and bewildered by her absence, they ran wild. Some fled into the forest and perished. A few survived, along with the many street dogs that proliferate around the hill station.

If you see a dog that looks especially weird (bits of terrier, spaniel, Pom and dachshund), you'll know it's descended from one of Mrs Roberts' pets. She did leave us a legacy of sorts.

NON-FICTION

LIFE AT MY OWN PACE

All my life I've been a walking person. To this day I have neither owned nor driven a car, bus, tractor, aeroplane, motor boat, scooter, truck, or steamroller. Forced to make a choice, I would drive a steamroller, because of its slow but solid progress and unhurried finality.

In my early teens I did for a brief period ride a bicycle, until I rode into a bullock cart and broke my arm; the accident only serving to underline my unsuitability for any wheeled conveyance that is likely to take my feet off the ground. Although dreamy and absent-minded, I have never *walked* into a bullock cart.

Perhaps there is something to be said for sun signs. Mine being Taurus, I have, like the bull, always stayed close to grass, and have lived my life at my own leisurely pace only being stirred into furious activity when goaded beyond endurance. I have every sympathy for bulls and none for bullfighters.

I was born in the Kasauli military hospital in 1934, and was baptized in the little Anglican church which still stands in the hill station. My father had done his schooling at the Lawrence Royal Military School, at Sanawar, a few miles away, but he had gone into 'tea' and then teaching, and at the time I was born he was out of a job. In any case, the only hospital in Kasauli was the Pasteur Institute for the treatment of rabies, and as neither of my parents had been bitten by a mad dog, it was the army who took charge of my delivery.

But my earliest memories are not of Kasauli, for we left when I was two or three months old; they are of Jamnagar, a small state in coastal Kathiawar, where my father took a job as English tutor to several young princes and princesses. This was in the tradition of Forster and Ackerley, but my father did not have literary ambitions, although after his death I was to come across a notebook filled with love poems addressed to my mother, presumably written while they were courting.

This was where the walking really began, because Jamnagar was full of palaces and spacious lawns and gardens, and by the time I was three I was exploring much of this territory on my own, with the result that I encountered my first cobra, who, instead of striking me dead as the best fictional cobras are supposed to do, allowed me to pass.

Living as he did so close to the ground, and sensitive to every footfall, that intelligent snake must have known instinctively that I presented no threat, that I was just a small human discovering the use of his legs. Envious of the snake's swift gliding movements, I went indoors and tried crawling about on my belly, but I wasn't much good at it. Legs were better.

Amongst my father's pupils from one of these small states were three beautiful princesses. One of them was about my age, but the other two were older, and they were the ones at whose feet I worshipped. I think I was four or five when I had this strong crush on two 'older' girls—eight and ten respectively. At first I wasn't sure that they were girls because they always wore jackets and trousers and kept their hair quite short. But my father told me they were girls, and he never lied to me.

My father's schoolroom and our own living quarters were located in one of the older palaces, situated in the midst of a veritable jungle of a garden. Here I could roam to my heart's content, amongst marigolds and cosmos growing rampant in the long grass, an ayah or a bearer often being sent post-haste after me, to tell me to beware of snakes and scorpions.

One of the books read to me as a child was a work called *Little Henry and His Bearer,* in which little Henry converts his servant to Christianity. I'm afraid something rather different happened to me. My ayah, bless her soul, taught me to eat paan and other forbidden delights from the bazaar, while the bearer taught me to abuse in choice Hindustani—an attribute that has stood over the years.

Neither of my parents were overly religious, and religious tracts came my way far less frequently than they do now. (*Little Henry* was a gift from a distant aunt.) Nowadays, everyone seems to feel I have a soul worth saving, whereas, when I was a boy, I was left severely alone by both preachers and adults. In fact, the only time I felt threatened by religion was a few years later, when, visiting the aunt I have mentioned, I happened to fall down her steps and sprain my ankle. She gave me a triumphant look and said, 'See what happens when you don't go to church!'

My father was a good man. He taught me to read and write long before I started going to school, although it's true to say that I first learned to read *upside-down*. This happened because I would sit on a stool in front of the three princesses, watching them read and write and so the view I had of their books was an upside-down view; I still read that way occasionally, when a book gets boring.

He gave me books like *Peter Pan* and *Alice's Adventures in Wonderland* (which I lapped up); he was a fanatical stamp collector, had dozens of albums, and corresponded and dealt regularly with Stanley Gibbons in London. After he died, the collections disappeared; otherwise I might well have been left a fortune in rare stamps!

My mother was at least twelve years younger to my father and liked going out to parties and dances. She was quite happy to leave me in the care of the ayah and bearer. I had no objection to the arrangement. The servants indulged me; and so did my father, bringing me books, toys, comics, chocolates, and, of course, stamps, when he returned from visits to Bombay.

Walking along the beach, collecting seashells, I got into the habit of staring hard at the ground, a habit which has stayed with me all my life. Apart from helping my thought process, it also results in my picking up odd objects—coins, keys, broken bangles, marbles, pens, bits of crockery, pretty stones, ladybirds, feathers, snail-shells. Occasionally, of course, this habit results in my walking some way past my destination (if I happen to have one), and why not? It simply means discovering a new and different destination, sights and sounds that I might not have experienced had I ended my walk exactly where it was supposed to end. And I am not looking at the ground all the time. Sensitive like the snake to approaching footfalls I look up from time to time to examine the faces of passers-by, just in case they have something they wish to say to me.

A bird singing in a bush or tree has my immediate attention; so does any unfamiliar flower or plant, particularly if it grows in an unusual place such as a crack in the wall or rooftop, or in a yard full of junk where I once found a rose bush blooming on the roof of an old Ford car.

There are other kinds of walks that I shall come to later, but it wasn't until I came to Dehradun and my grandmother's house that I really found my feet as a walker.

In 1939, when World War II broke out, my father joined the RAF, and my mother and I went to stay with her mother in Dehradun, while my father found himself in a tent on the outskirts of Delhi.

It took two or three days by train from Jamnagar to Dehradun, but trains were not quite as crowded then as they are today (the population being much smaller), and provided no one got sick, a long train journey was something of an extended picnic, with halts at quaint little stations, railway meals in abundance brought by waiters in smart uniforms, an ever-changing landscape, bridges over mighty rivers, forest, desert, farmland, everything sun-drenched, the air clear and unpolluted except when dust storms swept across the plains. Bottled drinks were a rarity then, the occasional lemonade or 'Vimto' being the only aerated soft drinks, apart from soda water. We made our own orange juice or lime juice and took it with us.

By journey's end we were wilting and soot-covered, but Dehra's bracing winter climate brought us back to life.

Scarlet poinsettia leaves and trailing bougainvillaea adorned the garden walls, while in the compounds grew mangoes, litchis, papayas, guavas, and lemons large and small. It was a popular place for retiring Anglo-Indians, and my maternal grandfather, after retiring from the Railways, had built a neat, compact bungalow on the Old Survey Road. There it stands today, unchanged except in ownership. Dehra was a small, quiet garden-town, only parts of which are still recognizable, forty years after I first saw it.

I remember waking in the train early in the morning, and looking out of the window at heavy forest, trees of every description, but mostly sal and shisham; here and there a forest glade, or a stream of clear water—quite different from the muddied waters of the streams and rivers we'd crossed the previous day. As we passed over a largish river (the Sone) we saw a herd of elephants bathing; and leaving the forests of the Shivalik hills, we entered the Doon valley where fields of rice and flowering mustard stretched away to the foothills.

Outside the station we climbed into a tonga, and rolled creakingly along quiet roads until we reached my grandfather's house. Grandfather had died a couple of years previously, and Grandmother had lived alone, except for occasional visits from her married daughters and their families, and from the unmarried but wandering son Ken, who would turn up from time to time, especially when his funds were low. Granny also had a tenant, Miss Kellner, who occupied a portion of the bungalow.

Miss Kellner had been crippled in a carriage accident in Calcutta when she was a girl, and had been confined to a chair all her adult life. She had been left some money by her parents, and was able to afford an ayah and four stout palanquin-bearers, who carried her about when she wanted the chair moved and took her for outings in a real sedan-chair or sometimes a rickshaw—she had both. Her hands were deformed and she could scarcely hold a pen, but she managed to play cards quite dexterously and taught me a number of card games, which I have forgotten now, as Miss Kellner was the only person with whom I *could* play cards, as she allowed me to cheat. She took a fancy to me, and told Granny that I was the only one of her grandchildren with whom she could hold an intelligent conversation; Granny said that I was merely adept at flattery. It's true. Miss Kellner's cook made marvellous meringues, coconut biscuits, and curry puffs, and these would be used very successfully to lure me over to her side of the garden, where she was usually to be found sitting in the shade of an old mango tree, shuffling her deck of cards. Granny's cook made a good kofta curry, but he did not go in for the exotic trifles that Miss Kellner served up.

Granny employed a full-time gardener, a wizened old character named Dukhi (sad), and I don't remember that he ever laughed or smiled. I'm not sure what deep tragedy dwelt behind those dark eyes (he never spoke about himself, even when questioned) but he was tolerant of me, and talked to me about flowers and their characteristics.

There were rows and rows of sweet peas; beds full of phlox and sweet-smelling snapdragons; geraniums on the veranda steps, hollyhocks along the garden wall... Behind the house were the fruit trees, somewhat neglected since my grandfather's death, and it was here that I liked to wander in the afternoons, for the old orchard was dark and private and full of possibilities. I made friends with an old jackfruit tree, in whose trunk was a large hole in which I stored marbles, coins, catapults, and other treasures much as a crow stores the bright objects it picks up during its peregrinations.

I have never been a great tree-climber, having a tendency to fall off the branches, but I liked climbing walls (and still do), and it was not long before I had climbed the wall behind the orchard, to drop into unknown territory and explore the bazaars and by-lanes of Dehra.

❧

'Great, grey, formless India,' as Kipling had called it, was, until I was eight or nine, unknown territory for me, and I had heard only vaguely of the freedom movement and Nehru and Gandhi; but then, a child of today's India is just as vague about them. Most domiciled Europeans and Anglo-Indians were apolitical. That the rule of the sahib was not exactly popular in the land was made plain to me on the few occasions I ventured far from the house. Shouts of 'Red Monkey!' or 'White Pig!' were hurled at me with some enthusiasm but without any physical follow-up. I had the sense, even then, to follow the old adage, 'Sticks and stones may break my bones, but words can never hurt me.'

It was a couple of years later, when I was eleven, just a year or two before Independence, that two passing cyclists, young men, swept past and struck me over the head. I was stunned but not hurt. They rode away with cries of triumph—I suppose it was a rare achievement to have successfully assaulted someone whom they associated with the ruling race—but although I could hardly (at that age) be expected to view them with Gandhian love and tolerance, I did not allow the resentment to rankle. I know I did not mention the incident to anyone—not to my mother or grandmother, or even to Mr Ballantyne, the SP (superintendent of police), a family friend who dropped in at the house quite frequently. Perhaps it was personal pride that prevented me from doing so; or perhaps I had already learnt to accept the paradox that India could be as cruel as it could be kind.

With my habit already formed, of taking long walks into unfamiliar areas, I exposed myself more than did most Anglo-Indian boys of my age. Boys bigger than me rode bicycles; boys smaller than me stayed at home!

My parent's marriage had been on the verge of breaking up, and I was eight or nine when they finally separated. My mother was soon married again, to a Punjabi businessman, while I went to join my father in his air force hutment in Delhi. I would return to Dehra, not once but many times in the course of my life, for the town, even when it ceased to enchant, continued to exert a considerable influence on me, both as a writer and as a person; not a literary influence (for that came almost entirely from books) but as an area whose atmosphere was to become a part of my mind and sensuous nature.

I had a very close relationship with my father and was more than happy with him in Delhi, although he would be away almost every day and sometimes, when he was hospitalized with malaria, he would be away almost every night too. When he was free, he took me for long walks to the old tombs and monuments that dotted the wilderness that then surrounded New Delhi; or to the bookshops and cinemas of Connaught Place, the capital's smart shopping complex, then spacious and uncluttered. I shared his fondness for musicals, and wartime Delhi had a number of cinemas offering all the glitter of Hollywood.

I wasn't doing much reading then—I did not, in fact, become a great reader until after my father's death—but played gramophone records when I was alone in the house, or strolled about the quiet avenues of New Delhi, waiting for my father to return from work. There was very little traffic in those days, and the roads were comparatively safe.

I was lonely, shy and aloof, and when other children came my way I found it difficult to relate to them. Not that they came my way very often. My father hadn't the time or the inclination to socialize and in the evening he would sit down to his stamp collection, while I helped to sort, categorize and mount his treasures.

I was quite happy with this life. During the day, when there was nothing else to do, I would make a long list of films or books or records; and although I have long since shed this hobby, it had the effect of turning me into an efficient cataloguer. When I became a writer, the world lost a librarian or archivist.

My father felt that this wasn't the right sort of life for a growing boy, and arranged for me to go to a boarding school in Simla. As often happens, when the time approached for me to leave, I did make friends with some other boys who lived down the road.

Trenches had been dug all over New Delhi in anticipation of Japanese air raids, and there were several along the length of the road on which we lived. These were ideal places for the games of cops and robbers, and I was gradually drawn into them. The heat of midsummer, with temperatures well over forty degrees Celsius, did not keep us indoors for long, and in any case the trenches were cooler than the open road. I discovered that I was quite strong too, in comparison with most boys of my age, and in the wrestling bouts that were often held in the trenches I invariably came out, quite literally, on top. At eight or nine I was a chubby boy; I hadn't learnt to use my fists (and never did), but I knew how to use my weight, and when I sat upon an opponent he usually remained sat upon until I decided to move.

I don't remember all their names, but there was a dark boy called Joseph, Goan I think, who was particularly nice to me, no matter how often I sat upon him. Our burgeoning friendship was cut short when my father and I set out for Simla. My father had two weeks' leave, and we could spend that time together before I was shut up in school. Ten years in a boarding school was to convince me that such places bring about an unnatural separation between children and parents that is good for neither body nor soul.

That fortnight with my father was the only happy spell in my life for some time to come. We walked up to the Hanuman temple on Jakke Hill; took a rickshaw ride to Sanjauli, while my father told me the story of Kipling's phantom rickshaw, set on that very road; ate ice creams at Davice's restaurant (and as I write this, I learn that this famous restaurant has just been destroyed in a fire); browsed in bookshops and saw more films; made plans for the future. 'We will go to England after the war.'

He was, in fact, the only friend I had as a child, and after his death I was to be a lonely boy until I reached my late teens.

School seemed a stupid and heartless place after my father had gone away. The traditions even in prep school—such as ragging and caning, compulsory games and daily chapel attendances, prefects larger than life, and honour boards for everything from school captaincy to choir membership—had apparently been borrowed from *Tom Brown's Schooldays*. It was all part of the process of turning us into 'leaders of men'. Well, my leadership qualities remained exactly at zero, and in time I was to discover the sad fact that the world at large judges you according to who you are, rather than what you have done.

My father had been transferred to Calcutta and wasn't sleeping well. Malaria again. And jaundice, but his last letter sounded quite cheerful. He'd been selling his valuable stamp collection, so as to have enough money for us to settle in England.

One day my class teacher sent for me.

'I want to talk to you, Bond,' he said. 'Let's go for a walk.'

I knew it wasn't going to be a walk I would enjoy; I knew instinctively that something was wrong.

As soon as my unfortunate teacher (no doubt cursing the headmaster for giving him such an unpleasant task) started on the theme of 'God wanting your father in a higher and better place'—as though there could be any better place than Jakke Hill in midsummer!—I knew my father was dead, and burst into tears.

Later, the headmaster sent for me and made me give him the pile of letters from my father that I had been keeping in my locker. He probably felt it was unmanly of me to cling to them.

'You might lose them,' he said. 'Why not keep them with me? At the end of the term, before you go home, you can come and collect them.'

Reluctantly I gave him the letters. He told me he had heard from my mother and stepfather and that I would be going to them when school closed.

At the end of the year, the day before school closed, I went to the HM's office and asked him for my letters.

'What letters?' he said. His desk was piled with papers and correspondences, and he was irritated by the interruption.

'My father's letters,' I explained. 'You said you would keep them for me, sir.'

'Letters, letters. Are you sure you gave them to me?' He was growing more irritated. 'You must be mistaken, Bond. What would I want from your father's letters?'

'I don't know, sir. You said I could collect them before going home.'

'Look, I don't remember your letters and I'm very busy just now. So run along. I'm sure you're mistaken, but if I find any personal letters of yours, I'll send them to you.'

I don't suppose his forgetfulness was anything more than the muddled indifference that grows in many of those who have charge of countless small boys, but for the first time in my life, I knew what it was like to hate someone.

And I had discovered that words could hurt too.

A GOOD PHILOSOPHY

The other day, when I was with a group of students, a bright young thing asked me, 'Sir, what is your philosophy of life?' She had me stumped.

There I was, a seventy-five-year-old, still writing, and still functioning physically and mentally (or so I believed), but quite helpless when it came to formulating a 'philosophy of life'.

How dare I reach the venerable age of seventy-five without a philosophy; without anything resembling a religious outlook; without arming myself with a battery of great thoughts with which to impress my young interlocutor, who is obviously in need of a little practical if not spiritual guidance to help her navigate the shoals of life.

This morning I was pondering on this absence of a philosophy or religious outlook in my make-up, and feeling a little low because it was cloudy and dark outside, and gloomy weather always seems to dampen my spirits. Then the clouds broke up and the sun came out, large, yellow splashes of sunshine in my room and upon my desk, and almost immediately I felt an uplift of spirit. And at the same time I realized that no philosophy would be of any use to a person so susceptible to changes in light and shade, sunshine and shadow. I was a pagan, pure and simple; a sensualist, sensitive to touch and colour and fragrance and odour and sounds of every description; a creature of instinct, of spontaneous attractions, given to illogical fancies and attachments. As a guide, philosopher and friend I am of no use to anyone, least of all myself.

I think the best advice I ever had was contained in these lines from Shakespeare which my father had copied into one of my notebooks when I was nine years old:

This above all to thine own self be true,
And it must follow, as the night the day,
Thou canst not then be false to any man.

Each one of us is a mass of imperfections, and to be able to recognize and live with our imperfections, our basic natures, defects of genes and birth—hereditary flaws—makes for an easier transit on life's journey.

I am always a little weary of saints and godmen, preachers and teachers, who are ready with solutions for all our problems. For one thing, they talk too much. When I was at school, I mastered the art of sleeping (without appearing to sleep) through a long speech or lecture by the principal or visiting dignitary, and I must confess to doing the same thing today. The trick is to sleep with your eyes half closed; this gives the impression of concentrating very hard on what is being said, even though you might well be roaming happily in dreamland.

In our imperfect world there is far too much talk and not enough thought.

The TV channels are awash with TV gurus telling us how to live, and they do so at great length. This verbal diarrhoea is infectious and appears to affect newspersons and TV anchors who are prone to lecturing and bullying the guests on their show. Too many know-alls. A philosophy for living? You won't find it on your TV sets. You will learn more from a cab driver or street vendor.

'And what's your philosophy?' I asked my sabziwala, as he weighed out a kilo of onions.

'Philosophy? What's that?' He turned to his assistant. 'Is this gentleman trying to abuse me?'

'No sir,' I said. 'It's not a term of abuse. I was just asking—are you a happy man?'

'Why do you want to know? Are you from the income tax department?'

'No, I'm just a storyteller. So tell me—what makes you happy?'

'A good customer,' he said. 'So tell me what makes *you* happy?'

'The same thing, I suppose,' I had to confess. 'A good publisher!'

I did not tell him about the sunshine, the birdsong, the bedside book, the potted geranium, and all the other little things that make life worth living. It's better that he finds out for himself.

GREAT TREES OF GARHWAL

Living for many years in a cottage at 7,000 feet in the Garhwal Himalayas, I was fortunate to have a big window that opened out to the forest, so that the trees were almost within my reach. Had I jumped, I should have landed quite safely in the arms of an oak or chestnut.

The incline of the hill was such that my first-floor window opened on what must, I suppose, have been the second floor of the tree. I never made the jump, but the big langurs—silver-grey monkeys with long swishing tails—often leapt from the trees onto the corrugated tin roof and made enough noise to disturb the bats sleeping in the space between the roof and ceiling.

Standing on its own was a walnut tree, and truly this was a tree for all seasons. In winter, the branches were bare; but they were smooth and straight and round like the arms of a woman in a painting by Jamini Roy. In the spring, each branch produced a hard, bright spear of new leaf. By midsummer the entire tree was in leaf, and towards the end of the monsoon, the walnuts, encased in their green jackets, had reached maturity.

Then the jackets began to split, revealing the hard brown shell of the walnuts. Inside the shell was the nut itself. Look closely at the nut and you will notice that it is shaped rather like the human brain. No wonder the ancients prescribed walnuts for headaches!

Every year the tree gave me a basket of walnuts. But last year the walnuts were disappearing one by one, and I was at a loss to know who had been taking them. Could it have been

Bijju, the milkman's son? He was an inveterate tree climber. But he was usually to be found on oak trees, gathering fodder for his cows. He told me that his cows like oak leaves but did not care for walnuts. He admitted that they had relished my dahlias, which they had eaten the previous week, but he denied having fed them walnuts.

It wasn't the woodpecker. He was out there every day, knocking furiously against the bark of the tree, trying to prise an insect out of a narrow crack. He was strictly non-vegetarian and none the worse for it.

One day I found a fat langur sitting in the walnut tree. I watched him for some time to see if he was going to help himself to the nuts, but he was only sunning himself. When he thought I wasn't looking he came down and ate the geraniums, but he did not take any walnuts.

The walnuts had been disappearing early in the morning while I was still in bed. So one morning I surprised everyone, including myself, by getting up before sunrise. I was just in time to catch the culprit climbing out of the walnut tree.

It was the old woman who sometimes came to cut grass on the hillside. Her face was as wrinkled as the walnuts she had been helping herself to. In spite of her age, her arms and legs were sturdy. When she saw, me she was as swift as a civet cat in getting out of the tree.

'And how many walnuts did you gather today, Grandmother?' I asked.

'Only two,' she said with a giggle, offering them to me on her open palm. I accepted one of them. Encouraged, she climbed back into the tree and helped herself to the remaining nuts. It was impossible to object. I was taken up in admiration of her agility in the tree. She must have been about sixty, and I was a mere forty-five, but I knew I would never be climbing trees again.

To the victor the spoils!

The horse chestnuts were inedible, even the monkeys threw them away in disgust. Once, on passing beneath a horse chestnut tree, a couple of chestnuts bounced off my head. Looking up, I saw that they had been dropped on me by a couple of mischievous rhesus monkeys.

The tree itself is a friendly one, especially in summer when it is in full leaf. The least breath of wind makes the leaves break into conversation, and their rustle is a cheerful sound, unlike the sad notes of pine trees in the wind. The spring flowers look like candelabra, and when the blossoms fall they carpet the hillside with their pale pink petals.

We pass now to my favourite tree, the deodar. In Garhwal and Kumaon it is called dujar or devdar; in Jaunsar and parts of Himachal it is known as the kelu or kelon. It is also identified with the cedar of Lebanon (the cones are identical), although the deodar's needles are slightly longer and more bluish. Trees, like humans, change with their environment. Several persons familiar with the deodar at Indian hill stations, when asked to point it out in London's Kew Gardens, indicated the cedar of Lebanon; and when shown a deodar, declared that they had never seen this tree in the Himalayas!

We shall stick to the name deodar which comes from the Sanskrit Deva-daru (divine tree). It is a sacred tree in the Himalayas; not worshipped, not protected in the way that a pipal is in the plains, but sacred in that its timber has always been used in temples, for doors, windows, walls and even roofs. Quite frankly, I would just as soon worship the deodar as worship anything, for in its beauty and majesty it represents nature in its most noble aspect.

No one who has lived among deodars would deny that it is the most godlike of Himalayan trees. It stands erect, dignified, and though in a strong wind it may hum and sigh and moan, it does not bend to the wind. The snow slips softly from its resilient branches. In the spring new leaves are tender green, while during the monsoon the tiny young cones spread like blossoms in the dark green folds of the branches. The deodar thrives in the rain and enjoys the company of its own kind. Where one deodar grows, there will be others. Isolate a young tree and it will often pine away.

The great deodar forests are found along the upper reaches of the Bhagirathi valley and the Tons in Garhwal; and in Himachal and Kashmir, along the Chenab and Jhelum, and also the Kishanganga; it is at its best between 7,000 and 9,000 feet. I had expected to find it in the upper reaches of Alaknanda, but could not find a single deodar along the road to Badrinath. That particular valley seems hostile to trees in general, and deodars in particular.

The average girth of the deodar is 15-20 feet, but individual trees often attain a great size. Records show that one great deodar was 250 feet high, 20 feet in girth at the base, and more than 550 years old.

The timber of these trees, which is unaffected by extremes of climate, was always highly prized for house building; and in the village of Jaunsar Bawar, finely carved doors and windows are a feature of the timbered dwellings. Many of the quaint old bridges over the Jhelum in Kashmir are supported on pillars fashioned from whole deodar trees; some of these bridges are more than 500 years old.

※

To return to my own trees, I went among them often, acknowledging their presence with the touch of my hand against their trunks—the walnut's smooth and polished; the pine's patterned and whorled; and the oak's rough, gnarled, full of experience. The oak had been there the longest, and the winds had bent his upper branches and twisted a few, so that he looked shaggy and undistinguished. It is a good tree for the privacy of birds, its crooked branches spreading out with no particular effect; and sometimes the tree seems uninhabited until there is a whirring sound, as of a helicopter approaching, and a party of long-tailed blue magpies stream across the forest glade.

After the monsoon, when the dark red berries had ripened on the hawthorn, this pretty tree was visited by green pigeons, the kokla birds of Garhwal, who clambered upside down among the fruit-laden twigs. And during winter, a white-capped redstart perched on the bare branches of the wild pear tree and whistled cheerfully. He had come down from higher places to winter in the garden.

The pines grow on the next hill—the chir, the Himalayan blue pine, and the long-leaved pine—but there is a small blue pine a little way below the cottage, and sometimes I sit beneath it to listen to the wind playing softly on its branches.

Open the window at night and there is usually something to listen to—the mellow whistle of a pygmy owlet, or the cry of a barking deer which has scented the proximity of a panther. Sometimes, if you are lucky, you will see the moon coming up over Nag Tibba and two distant deodars in perfect silhouette.

Some sounds cannot be recognized. They are strange night sounds, the sounds of the trees themselves, stretching their limbs in the dark, shifting a little, flexing their fingers. Great trees of the mountains, they know me well. They know my face in the window; they see me watching them, watching them grow, listening to their secrets, bowing my head before their outstretched arms and seeking their benediction.

A NIGHT WALK HOME

No night is so dark as it seems.

Here in Landour, on the first range of the Himalayas, I have grown accustomed to the night's brightness—moonlight, starlight, lamplight, firelight! Even fireflies light up the darkness.

Over the years, the night has become my friend. On the one hand, it gives me privacy; on the other, it provides me with limitless freedom.

Not many people relish the dark. There are some who will even sleep with their lights burning all night. They feel safer that way. Safer from the phantoms conjured up by their imagination. A primeval instinct, perhaps, going back to the time when primitive man hunted by day and was in turn hunted by night.

And yet, I have always felt safer by night, provided I do not deliberately wander about on clifftops or roads where danger is known to lurk. It's true that burglars and lawbreakers often work by night, their principal objective being to get into other people's houses and make off with the silver or the family jewels. They are not into communing with the stars. Nor are late-night revellers, who are usually to be found in brightly lit places and are thus easily avoided. The odd drunk stumbling home is quite harmless and probably in need of guidance.

I feel safer by night, yes, but then I do have the advantage of living in the mountains, a region where crime and random violence are comparatively rare. I know that if I were living in a big city in some other part of the world, I would think twice about walking home at midnight, no matter how pleasing the night sky was.

Walking home at midnight in Landour can be quite eventful, but in a different sort of way. One is conscious all the time of the silent life in the surrounding trees and bushes. I have smelt a leopard without seeing it. I have seen jackals on the prowl. I have watched foxes dance in the moonlight. I have seen flying squirrels flit from one treetop to another. I have observed pine martens on their nocturnal journeys, and listened to the calls of the nightjars and owls and other birds who live by night. Not all on the same night, of course. That would be a case of too many riches all at once. Some night walks can be uneventful. But usually there is something to see or hear or sense. Like those foxes dancing in the moonlight. One night, when I got home, I sat down and wrote these lines:

> As I walked home last night,
> I saw a lone fox dancing
> In the bright moonlight.
> I stood and watched; then
> Took the low road, knowing
> The night was by his right.
> Sometimes when words ring true.
> I'm like a lone fox dancing
> In the morning dew.

Who else, apart from foxes, flying squirrels and night-loving writers are at home in the dark? Well, there are the nightjars, not much to look at, although their large, lustrous eyes gleam uncannily in the light of a lamp. But their sounds are distinctive. The breeding call of the Indian nightjar resembles the sound of a stone skimming over the surface of a frozen pond—it can be heard for a considerable distance. Another species utters a loud grating call which, when close at hand, sounds exactly like a whiplash cutting through the air. Horsfield's nightjar (with which I am more familiar in Mussoorie) makes a noise similar to that made by striking a plank with a hammer.

I must not forget the owls. Those most celebrated of night birds, much maligned by those who fear the night. Most owls have very pleasant calls. The little jungle owlet has a note that is both mellow and musical. One misguided writer has likened its call to a motorcycle starting up, but this is libel. If only motorcycles sounded like the jungle owl, the world would be a more peaceful place to live and sleep in. Then there is the little scops owl, who speaks only in monosyllables, occasionally saying 'wow' softly but with great deliberation. He will continue to say 'wow' at intervals of about a minute, for several hours throughout the night.

Probably the most familiar of Indian owls is the spotted owlet, a noisy bird who pours forth a volley of chuckles and squeaks in the early evening and at intervals all night. Towards sunset, I watch the owlets emerge from their holes one after another. Before coming out, each puts out a queer little round head with staring eyes. After they have emerged they usually sit very quietly for a time as though only half awake. Then, all of a sudden, they begin to chuckle, finally breaking out into a torrent of chattering. Having in this way 'psyched' themselves into the right frame of mind, they spread their short, rounded wings and sail off for the night's hunting.

And I wend my way homewards. 'Night with her train of stars' is always enticing. The poet Henley found her so. But he also wrote of 'her great gift of sleep', and it is this gift that I am now about to accept with gratitude and humility.

A FRIGHT IN THE NIGHT

Our elderly school nurse, Miss Babcock, passed away quite suddenly one autumn evening, apparently of a heart attack. She was laid out on her camp bed in the little room adjoining our four-bed hospital ward. The funeral would be held next day.

Tata and I were school prefects that year, and we both knew Miss Babcock quite well, having often feigned stomach aches or sore throats in order to escape morning PT (physical training) or extra maths periods. It wasn't really a hospital, just a sick bay for the usual cases of measles or mumps. Anyone who went down with something really serious would be sent to Simla's Ripon Hospital.

Mr Fisher, our headmaster, summoned Tata and me to his office.

'Bond,' he said. 'You liked Miss Babcock, didn't you?'

'Yes, sir.'

'And you, Tata?'

'She was a good sport, sir.'

'Good. And since you are both familiar with the hospital, having got yourselves admitted whenever possible, I think it only right that you should be given the duty of keeping a vigil for Miss Babcock. It's not good to leave the dead alone all night. All you have to do is spend the night beside her bed. Keep the rats away! You can take turns. From nine to midnight, Bond will be on duty. After that, Tata will take over. There's a spare bed in the ward, and an easy chair in the bedroom. Now have your supper, and then go down to the hospital and relieve Mr Jones, who has been there all evening.'

Mr Jones was happy to be able to return to arranging his stamp collection, and wished us a comfortable night in the company of Miss Babcock.

The old lady looked peaceful enough stretched out on her camp bed. She was covered in a bedsheet and only her face and hands were visible. Someone had tried to close her eyes but they remained only half shut.

'Don't try anything funny,' said Tata. 'I think she's watching us.'

'She's been dead for hours,' I said. 'You go and lie down. I'll wake you up at twelve.'

Tata returned to the ward, and I sat down in the easy chair near Miss Babcock's bed. It was a still, silent night, the only sound being the ticking of a wall clock in a corner of the room. A small light bulb glowed over the dressing table. But in those days we were subject to power failures just as we are today, and presently the bulb went out and we were plunged into darkness.

But not for long.

Presently, a full moon came up over the mountains, flooding the garden with moonlight. A moonbeam crept in at the window and moved slowly across the room. Outside, a nightjar honked.

I had been watching Miss Babcock's peaceful countenance for some time, wondering if her spirit was hovering around the room, keeping a watch over me even as I kept a watch over her. In the dark I could only make out the outline of her face, but as the moonlight crept across her bed, I began to make out her features.

Presently the moonlight rested on her face. I could see all her features quite distinctly.

And then, to my horror, she began to smile at me.

A corpse smiling at you in the middle of the night is not the most pleasant of experiences. It is calculated to give you goosebumps. And when the smile becomes an evil grimace, it is time to say your prayers.

But there was no time for prayer. The smile widened even further, and then, with a loud bang—somewhat like a firecracker going off—Miss Babcock's set of false teeth shot out of her mouth and landed on the bedsheet.

At the same time I shot out of my chair and fled from the room, calling to Tata for help.

'She's alive!' I cried. 'Miss Babcock's after me!'

Tata leapt out of bed, peeked into Miss Babcock's room, saw her grinning face, and came back shouting, 'Let's get Fishy!' ('Fishy' being short for our headmaster, Mr Fisher.) 'Before she starts screaming at us!'

Together we rushed up the hospital steps and down the path to the headmaster's house. The headmaster dragged Mr Jones away from his stamp collection, and the four of us tramped down to the hospital, fully expecting to find Miss Babcock walking about.

But she was still laid out, and still very much dead—according to Mr Jones, who'd been in the army and seen many dead people.

'We forgot to take her teeth out,' he explained, indicating Miss Babcock's false teeth which had popped out during my vigil. 'When rigor mortis set in, and her jaw stiffened, the teeth were forced out.'

'They came out with a lot of noise, sir,' I said, still shaken up. 'And she was grinning at me all the time.'

'Well, we know you're a funny fellow, Bond,' said Mr Fisher, giving me one of his own sarcastic smiles. 'Even a corpse can't help grinning at you!'

Tata and I were excused from further 'invigilation', and sent back to our dormitories, where we regaled everyone with a hair-raising account of our experience.

This is a perfectly true story, but it is not really a ghost story.

I think I would prefer seeing a ghost to sitting up with a corpse late into the night.

BIRDSONG IN THE HILLS

Birdwatching is more difficult in the hills than on the plains. Many birds are difficult to spot against the dark green of the trees or the varying shades of the hillsides. Large gardens and open fields make birdwatching much easier on the plains; but up here in the mountains one has to be quick of eye to spot a flycatcher flitting from tree to tree, or a mottled brown treecreeper ascending the trunk of oak or spruce. But few birds remain silent, and one learns of their presence from their calls or songs. Birdsong is with you wherever you go in the hills, from the foothills to the tree line; and it is often easier to recognize a bird from its voice than from its colourful but brief appearance.

The barbet is one of those birds which are heard more than they are seen. Summer visitors to our hill stations must have heard their monotonous, far-reaching call, 'pee-oh, pee-oh or un-neeow, un-neeow'. They would probably not have seen the birds, as they keep to the tops of high trees, where they are not easily distinguished from the foliage. Apart from that, the sound carries for about half a mile, and as the bird has the habit of turning its head from side to side while calling, it is very difficult to know in which direction to look for it.

Barbets love listening to their own voices and often two or three birds answer each other from different trees, each trying to outdo the other in a shrill shouting match. Most birds are noisy during the mating season. Barbets are noisy all the year round!

Some people like the barbet's call and consider it both striking and pleasant. Some don't like it and simply consider it striking!

In parts of the Garhwal Himalayas there is a legend that the bird is the reincarnation of a moneylender who died of grief at the unjust termination of a lawsuit. Eternally his plaint rises to heaven, 'un-neeow, un-neeow' which means 'injustice, injustice'.

Barbets are found throughout the tropical world, but probably the finest of these birds is the great Himalayan barbet. Just over a foot in length, it has a massive yellow bill, almost as large as that of a toucan. The head and neck are a rich violet, the upper back is olive brown with pale green streaks. The wings are green, washed with blue, brown and yellow. In spite of all these brilliant colours, the barbet is not easily distinguished from its leafy surroundings. It goes for the highest treetops and seldom comes down to earth.

Hodgson's grey-headed flycatcher-warbler is the long name that ornithologists, in their infinite wisdom, have given to a very small bird. This tiny bird is heard, if not seen, more often than any other bird throughout the Western Himalayas. It is almost impossible to visit any hill station between Nainital and Dalhousie without noticing this warbler; its voice is heard in every second tree, and yet there are few who can say what it looks like.

Its song (if you can call it that) is not very musical, and Douglas Dewar in writing about it was reminded of a notice that once appeared in a third-rate music hall: 'The audience is respectfully requested not to throw things at the pianist. He is doing his best.'

Our little warbler does his best, incessantly emitting four or five unmusical but joyful and penetrating notes.

He is much smaller than a sparrow, being only some four inches in length, of which one-third consists of tail. His lower plumage is bright yellow, his upper parts olive green; the head and neck are grey, the head being set off by cream-coloured eyebrows. He is an active little bird always on the move, and both he and his mate, sometimes a few friends, hop about from leaf to leaf, looking for insects both large and small. And the way he puts away an inch-long caterpillar would please the most accomplished spaghetti eater!

Another tiny bird heard more often than it is seen is the green-backed tit, a smart little bird about the size of a sparrow. It constantly utters a sharp, rather metallic but not unpleasant, call that sounds like 'kiss me, kiss me, kiss me...'

The sunbird, which is found in Kumaon and Garhwal, is also a fine singer. But perhaps the best songster of the lot is the grey-winged ouzel. Throughout the early summer he makes the wooded hillsides ring with his blackbird-like melody. The hill people call this bird the kastura or kasturi, a name also applied to the Himalayan whistling thrush. But the whistling thrush has a yellow bill, whereas the ouzel is red-billed and is much the sweeter singer.

Nightjars (or goatsuckers, to give them their ancient name) are birds that lie concealed during the day in shady woods, coming out at dusk on silent wings to hunt for insects. The nightjar has a huge frog-like mouth, but is best recognized by its long tail and wings and its curiously silent flight. After dusk and just before dawn, you can hear its curious call, 'tonk-tonk, tonk-tonk', a note like that produced by striking a plank with a hammer.

As we pass from the plains to the hills, the traveller is transported from one bird realm to another.

Rajpur is separated from Mussoorie by a five-mile footpath, and within that brief distance we find the caw of the house crow replaced by the deeper note of the corby. Instead of the crescendo shriek of the koel, the double note of the cuckoo meets the ear. For the eternal cooing of the little brown dove, the melodious kokla green pigeon is substituted. The harsh cries of the rose-ringed parakeets give place to the softer call of the slate-headed species. The dissonant voices of the seven sisters no longer issue from the bushes; their place is taken by the weird but more pleasing calls of the Himalayan streaked laughingthrushes.

When I first came to live in the hills, it was the song of the

Himalayan whistling thrush that caught my attention. I did not see the bird that day. It kept to the deep shadows of the ravine below the old stone cottage.

The following day I was sitting at my window, gazing out at the new leaves on the walnut and wild pear trees. All was still, the wind was at peace with itself, the mountains brooded massively under the darkening sky. And then, emerging from the depths of that sunless chasm like a dark, sweet secret, came the indescribably beautiful call of the whistling thrush.

It is a song that never fails to thrill and enchant me. The bird starts with a hesitant schoolboy whistle, as though trying out the tune; then, confident of the melody, it bursts into full song, a crescendo of sweet notes and variations that ring clearly across the hillside. Suddenly the song breaks off right in the middle of a cadenza, and I am left wondering what happened to make the bird stop so suddenly.

At first the bird was heard but never seen. Then one day I found the whistling thrush perched on the broken garden fence. He was a deep glistening purple, his shoulders flecked with white; he had sturdy black legs and a strong yellow beak. A dapper fellow who would have looked just right in a top hat! When he saw me coming down the path, he uttered a sharp 'kree-ee'—unexpectedly harsh when compared to his singing—and flew off into the shadowed ravine.

As the months passed, he grew used to my presence and became less shy. Once the rainwater pipes were blocked, and this resulted in an overflow of water and a small permanent puddle under the steps. This became the whistling thrush's favourite bathing place. On sultry summer afternoons, while I was taking a siesta upstairs, I would hear the bird flapping about in the rainwater pool. A little later, refreshed and sunning himself on the roof, he would treat me to a little concert—performed, I could not help feeling, especially for my benefit.

It was Govind, the milkman, who told me the legend of

the whistling thrush, which the hill people call Krishna-patti (in addition to kastura).

According to the story, Lord Krishna fell asleep near a mountain stream and while he slept, a small boy made off with the god's famous flute. Upon waking and finding his flute gone, Krishna was so angry that he changed the culprit into a bird. But having once played on the flute, the bird had learnt bits and pieces of Krishna's wonderful music. And so he continued, in his disrespectful way, to play the music of the gods, only stopping now and then (as the whistling thrush does) when he couldn't remember the tune.

It wasn't long before my whistling thrush was joined by a female, who looked exactly like him. (I am sure there are subtle points of difference, but not to my myopic eyes!) Sometimes they gave solo performances, sometimes they sang duets; and these, no doubt, were love calls, because it wasn't long before the pair were making forays into the rocky ledges of the ravine, looking for a suitable maternity home. But a few breeding seasons were to pass before I saw any of their young.

After almost three years in the hills, I came to the conclusion that these were 'birds for all seasons'. They were liveliest in midsummer, but even in the depths of winter, with snow lying on the ground, they would suddenly start singing as they flitted from pine to oak to naked chestnut.

As I write, there is a strong wind rushing through the trees and bustling about in the chimney, while distant thunder threatens a storm. Undismayed, the whistling thrushes are calling to each other as they roam the wind-threshed forest.

Whistling thrushes usually nest on rocky ledges near water, but my overture of friendship may have given my visitors other ideas. Recently I was away from Mussoorie for about a fortnight. When I returned, I was about to open the window when I noticed a large bundle of ferns, lichen, grass, mud and moss balanced outside on the window ledge. Peering through the glass, I was able to recognize this untidy bundle as a nest.

It meant, of course, that I couldn't open the window, as this would have resulted in the nest toppling over the edge. Fortunately, the room had another window and I kept this one open to let in sunshine, fresh air, the music of birds, and, always welcome, the call of the postman! The postman's call may not be as musical as birdsong, but this writer never tires of it, for it heralds the arrival of the occasional cheque that makes it possible for him to live close to nature.

And now, this very day, three pink freckled eggs lie in the cup of moss that forms the nursery in this jumble of a nest. The parent birds, both male and female, come and go, bustling about very efficiently, fully prepared for a great day that's coming soon.

The wild cherry tree, which I grew especially for birds, attracts a great many small birds, both when it is in flower and when it is in fruit.

When it is covered with pale pink blossoms, the most common visitor is a little yellow-backed sunbird, who emits a squeaky little song as he flits from branch to branch. He extracts the nectar from the blossoms with his tubular tongue, sometimes while hovering on the wing but usually while clinging to the slender twigs.

Just as some vegetarians will occasionally condescend to eat meat, the sunbird (like the barbet) will vary his diet with insects. Small spiders, caterpillars, beetles, bugs and flies (probably in most cases themselves visitors to these flowers) fall prey to these birds. I have also seen a sunbird flying up and catching insects on the wing.

The flycatchers are gorgeous birds, especially the paradise flycatcher with its long white tail and ghostlike flight; and although they are largely insectivorous, like some meat-eaters they will also take a little fruit! And so they will occasionally visit the cherry tree when its sour little cherries are ripening. While travelling over the boughs, they utter twittering notes with occasional louder calls, and now and then the male bird breaks out into a sweet little song, thus justifying the name of Shah bulbul by which he is known in northern India.

ONCE UPON A MOUNTAIN TIME

My solitude...is not my own, for I see now how much it belongs to them—and that I have a responsibility for it in their regard not just in my own. It is because I am one with them that I owe it to them to be alone, and when I am alone they are not 'they' but my own self. There are no strangers.

From *Conjectures of a Guilty Bystander*—Thomas Merton

The trees stand watch over my day-to-day life. They are the guardians of my conscience. I have no one else to answer to, so I live and work under the generous but highly principled supervision of the trees—especially the deodars, who stand on guard, unbending, tolerant, they have had to put with a great deal, their branches continually lopped for fuel and fodder. 'What would *they* think?' I ask myself on many an occasion. 'What would they like me to do?' And I do what *I* think they would approve of most!

Well, it's nice to have someone to turn to...

The leaves are a fresh pale green in the spring rain. I can look at the trees from my window—look down on them almost, because the window is on the first floor of the cottage, and the hillside runs away at a sharp angle into the ravine. The trees and I know each other quite intimately, and we have much to say to each other from time to time.

I do nearly all my writing at this window seat. The trees

watch over me as I write. Whenever I look up, they remind me that they are there. They are my best critics. As long as I am aware of their presence, I can try to avoid the trivial and the banal.

Ramesh, the son of the municipal cleaner, looms darkly in the doorway. He is a stunted boy with a large head, but has wide gentle eyes. His orange-coloured trousers brighten up the surrounding gloom.

'What do you want, Ramesh?'

'Newspapers.'

'To sell to the kabadi?'

'No. For wrapping my schoolbooks.'

'Well, take a few.' I give him half a dozen old newspapers, the headlines already look meaningless.

'Sit down and wait for it to stop raining.'

He sits awkwardly on a mora.

'And what is your cousin Vinod doing these days?' (Vinod is a good-looking ne'er-do-well who seldom does anything apart from hanging around cinema halls.)

'Nothing.'

'Doesn't he go to school?'

'He has stopped going to school. He got a job at fifty rupees a month, but he left after a week. He says he will join the army in September.'

The rain stops and Ramesh departs. The clouds begin to break up, the sun strikes the steep hill on my left. A woman is chopping up sticks. I hear the tinkle of cowbells. Water drips from a leaking drainpipe. And suddenly, clear and pure, the song of the whistling thrush emerges like a dark sweet secret from the depths of the ravine.

Bijju is back from school and is taking his parents' cattle out to graze. He sees me at the window and waves, then grabs his favourite cow Neelu by the tail and tells her to hurry up.

Bijju is twelve, a fair, good-looking Garhwali boy. His younger sister and brother are very pretty children. The father, an electrician, is a rather self-effacing man. The mother is a strong, hard woman. I have watched her on the hillside cutting grass. She has the muscular calves of a man, solid feet and heavy hands, but she is a handsome woman. They live in a rented outhouse further up the hill.

Bijju doesn't visit me very often. He is rather shy. But one day I looked out of the window and there he was in the branches of the oak tree, smiling at me rather hesitantly. We spoke to each other across the three or four yards that separate house from oak tree.

'If I jump, I can land in your tree,' I said.

'And if I jump I will be in your house,' said Bijju.

'Come on then, jump!'

But he shook his head. He was afraid of me. The tree was safe. He put his arms round the thickest branch and held himself close to it. He looked very right in the tree, as though he belonged there, in a house of glossy new leaves.

'Come on, jump!'

'*You* jump,' he said.

In the evening his sister brings the cows home. I meet her on the path above the house. She is only a year younger than Bijju, a very bonny girl who is going to be ravishingly beautiful when she grows up, if they don't marry her off too soon. She too has the same timid smile. But if these children are timid of humans, they are not afraid in the forest, and often wander far afield with Neelu the blue cow and others. (And S, who is eighteen and educated at an English-medium private school, wouldn't go alone into the forest if you paid him!) But the trees know their own. They will cherish the wild spirit and frighten the daylights out of the tame.

The whistling thrush is here, bathing in the rainwater puddle beneath the window. He loves this spot. So now, when there is no rain, I fill the puddle with water, just so that my favourite bird keeps coming.

His bath finished, he perches on a branch of the walnut tree. His glossy blue-black wings glitter in the sunshine. At any moment he will start singing.

Here he goes! He tries out the tune, whistling to himself, and then, confident of the notes, sends his thrilling, full-throated voice far over the forest. The song dies down, trembling, lingering in the air; starts again, joyfully, and then suddenly stops, as though the singer had forgotten the words of the tune.

Vinod, the ne'er-do-well, turns up with a friend, asking me to give them some work. They want to go to the pictures, but have no money.

'You can dig up this slope below the house,' I tell them. 'The soil is good for growing vegetables.'

This sounds too much like hard work for Vinod, who says, 'We'll come and do it tomorrow.'

'No, we'll do it now,' says his more enterprising friend, and to my surprise they set to work.

Now and then I look out of the window. They are digging away with fair enthusiasm.

After about half an hour, Vinod keeps sitting down for short rests, to the increasing irritation of his partner. They are soon snapping at each other. Vinod looks very funny when he sulks, because he has a snub nose, and somehow a snub nose and a ferocious expression only reminds me of Richmal Crompton's William. But the work gets done by evening and they are quite pleased with their earnings.

Bijju is right at the top of a big oak. The branches sway to his movements. He grins down at me and waves. The higher he is in the tree, the more confident he becomes. It is only when he is down on the ground that he becomes shy and speechless.

He has allowed the cows to wander, and presently his mother's deep voice can be heard calling, 'Neelu, Neelu!' (The other cows don't have names.) And then, 'Where is that wretched boy?'

Sir Edmund Gibson has come up. He spends the summer

in the big house just down the road. He is wheezing a lot and says he has water in his lungs—and who wouldn't, at the age of eighty-six.

'Ruskin, my advice to you,' he says, 'is never to live beyond the age of eighty.'

'Well, once ought to be enough, sir.'

He is a big man, but not as red in the face as he used to be. His Gurkha manservant, Tirlok, has to push him up the steep slope to my gate.

Sir Edmund was once the British Resident in the Kathiawar states. He knew my parents in Jamnagar, when I was just five or six. He is a bachelor and is looked after by his servants.

His farm at Ramgarh doesn't make any money and he will probably give it to his retainers.

When Sir Edmund was resident, he was once shot at from close range by a terrorist. The man took four shots and missed every time. He must have been a terrible shot, or perhaps the pistol was faulty, because Sir E presents a very large target.

He also treasures two letters from Mahatma Gandhi, which were written from prison.

'I liked Gandhi,' says Sir E. 'He had a sense of humour. No politician today has a sense of humour. They all take themselves far too seriously. But not Gandhi. He took his work seriously, but not himself. When I went to see him in prison, I asked him if he was comfortable and he smiled and said, 'Even if I was, I wouldn't admit it!'

Sir E's servant brings tea, but there isn't any milk. I think I have exhausted Bijju's supply.

Now it's dusk and the trees are very still, very quiet. Far away I can hear the 'chuk-chuk-chuk' of a nightjar. The lights on Landour hill come on, one by one. There is a whirr of wings as the king crows fly into the trees to roost for the night. A rustling in the dry leaves below the window. A snake? Field rats? Porcupines? It is now too dark to find out. The day has ended, and the trees move closer together in the dark.

We are treated to one of those spectacular electric storms which are fairly frequent at this time of the year, late spring or early summer. The clouds grow very dark, then send bolts of lightning sizzling across the sky, lighting up the entire range of mountains. When the storm is directly overhead, there is hardly a pause in the frequency of the lightning; it is like a bright light being switched on and off with barely a second's interruption.

John Lang, writing in Dickens's magazine *Household Words* in 1853 almost exactly 120 years ago, had this to say about one of our storms:

> I have seen a storm on the heights of Jura—such a storm as Lord Byron describes. I have seen lightning, and heard thunder in Australia; I have, off Tierra del Fuego, the Cape of Good Hope, and the coast of Java, kept watch in thunderstorms which have drowned in their roaring the human voice, and made everyone deaf and stupefied; but these storms are not to be compared with a thunderstorm at Mussoorie or Landour.

Forgotten today, Lang was a popular writer in the mid-nineteenth century. He was also a successful barrister, who represented the Rani of Jhansi in her litigation with the East India Company. He spent his last years in Mussoorie and was buried in the Camel's Back Cemetery. His grave proved to be almost as elusive as his book and I found it with some difficulty, overgrown with moss and periwinkle. Prem and I cleaned it up, until the inscription stood out quite clearly.

Prem won't come home on a stormy night like this. He is afraid of the dark, but more than that, he is afraid of thunderstorms. It is as though the gods are ganging up against him. So he will spend the night in the school quarters, where he is visiting his mother who is staying there with relatives.

In the morning he turns up with a sheepish grin, saying it

got very late and he didn't want to wake me of the middle in the night. I try to feign anger, but it is a gloriously fresh and spirited morning—impossible to feel angry. A strong breeze is driving the clouds away, and the sun keeps breaking through. The birds are particularly active. The king crows (who weren't here last year) seem to have taken up residence in the oaks. I don't know why they are called crows. They are slim elegant black birds, with long-forked tails, and their call, far from being a caw, is quite musical, though slightly metallic. The mynas are very busy, very noisy, looking for a nesting site in the roof. The babblers are raking over fallen leaves, snapping up absent-minded grasshoppers. Now and then, the whistling thrush bursts into song, and then all other bird sounds pale into insignificance. Bijju has taken his cows to pasture and now scrambles up the hill, heading for home; he is late for school, and this is why he is in a hurry. He waves to me.

Both he and Prem have the high cheekbones and the deep-set eyes of the hill people. Prem, of course, is tall and dark. Bijju is small and fair; but he will grow into a sturdy young fellow.

The rain has driven the scorpions out of their rocks and crevices. I found one sitting on a loaf of bread. Up came his sting when we disturbed him. Prem tipped him out on the veranda steps and he scurried off into the bushes. I do not kill insects and other small creatures if I can help it, but there is a limit to my hospitality. I spared a centipede yesterday even though, last year, I was bitten by one which had occupied the seat of my pyjamas. Our hill scorpions and centipedes are not as dangerous as those found in the plains, and probably the same can be said for the people.

Prem tells me that his uncle is immune to scorpion stings, and allows himself to be stung in order to demonstrate his immunity. Apparently, his mother was stung by a scorpion shortly before his birth!

Azure butterflies flit about the garden like flakes of sky.

Learnt two new words: bosky—wooded, bushy (bosky shadows); girding—jesting, jeering (girding schoolboys, girding monkeys).

Poor old Sir E is in a bad way. He has diarrhoea, and little or no control over the muscles that play a part in controlling the bowels. The Gurkha servant called me, and I went over with some tablets. Sir E looked quite exhausted and was panting from the exertion of walking from his bed to the toilet. The Gurkha is very good—gives Sir E his bath, dresses him, helps him on with his pyjamas.

Grateful for my alacrity in coming over with some medicine, Sir E offers me whisky-and-soda (the first time he has ever done this), and pours himself a stiff brandy. He dozes off now and then, but the laboured breathing won't stop. He is a tough old tree, but I think he is beginning to find his massive frame something of a burden.

I make an attempt at conversation. 'Were you at Oxford or Cambridge?'

'Oxford. I joined Oxford in 1905 and left in 1909. Came to India in 1910.'

He has an excellent memory, unlike Mr Biggs (a retired headmaster) who is ten years younger but will repeat the same story thrice in ten minutes.

'And when were you knighted?' I ask.

'1939 or 1940.'

He is too tired to do much talking. I let him doze off, and give my attention to the whisky. The log fire burns well, the flames cast their glow on Sir E's white hair and hanging jowls. The stertorous breathing grows in volume. He wakes up suddenly, complains that the fire is too hot; Tirlok opens the window. I finish the whisky; he doesn't offer another. It is supper time anyway, and I suggest soup and toast. 'Call me in the night if you have any trouble,' I say. He looks very grateful. The loneliness must press upon him a great deal.

I go out into the night. The trees are bending to a strong wind. From the foliage comes a deep sigh, the voice of leagues of trees sleeping and half disturbed in their sleep. The sky is clear, tremendous with stars.

For the first time this year I hear the barbet, a sure sign the summer is upon us. Its importunate cry carries far across the hills. It can keep this up for hours, like a beggar. Indeed, as we have seen, its plaint—'un-neow, un-neow!'—has been likened in the hills to that of the spirit of the village moneylender who died before he could collect his dues.

It is difficult to spot the barbet. It is a fat green bird (no bigger than a myna, but fatter), and is usually perched at the very top of a deodar or cypress.

The whistling thrush comes to bathe in the rainwater puddle. Sir E is much better and is sitting outside in the shade of an old oak. They are probably about the same age. What a rugged constitution this man must have; first to survive, as a young man, all those diseases such as cholera, typhoid, dysentery, malaria, even the plague, which carried off so many Europeans in India (including my father); and now, an old man, to live and battle with congested lungs, a bad heart, weak eyes, bad teeth, recalcitrant bowels, and god knows what else, and still be able to derive some pleasure from living. His old Hillman car is equally indestructible. But, like Sir E, it can't get up the hill anymore; he uses it only in Dehradun.

I think his longevity is due simply to the fact that he refuses to go to bed when he is unwell. No amount of diarrhoea, or water in his lungs, will prevent him from getting up, dressing, writing letters, or getting on with the latest Wodehouse (a contemporary of his) or *Blackwood's Edinburgh Magazine*, to which he has been subscribing for the last fifty years! He was pleased to find that some of my own essays were appearing in *Blackwood's*. Nothing will keep him from his four o'clock tea or his evening whisky-and-soda. He is determined, I am sure, to die in his chair, with all his clothes on. The thought of being taken unaware while still in his pyjamas must be something of a nightmare to him. (His favourite film, he once told me, was *They Died with Their Boots On*).

The cicadas are tuning up for their first summer concert. Even Mrs Biggs, who is hard of hearing, can hear them. Yesterday, I met her on the road above the cottage and exchanged pleasantries. Up at Wynberg the girls' choir was hard at practice.

'The girls are in good voice today,' I remarked.

'Oh, yes, Mr Bond,' she said, presuming I meant the cicadas. 'They do it with their legs, don't they?'

❦

A week in Delhi. It is still only early summer, but the heat almost knocks one over. Slept on a roof, along with thousands of mosquitoes. It cools off in the early hours, but only briefly, before the sun comes shouting over the rooftops. The dust lies thick on floors, leaves, books, people. May's golden dust!

Now, back in the hills, I am struck first of all by the silence. The house, too, makes itself felt. It has been here too long not to have acquired a personality of its own. It is not a cheerful-looking place, nor is it exactly gloomy. My bedroom is rather dark (because it faces the abrupt slope of the hillside), but there is a wild cherry growing just outside the window—a cherry tree which I nurtured ever since it was a tiny seedling, five or six years ago, and which has now grown so tall that the branches tap against the roof whenever there is a breeze. It is a funny sort of cherry because it flowers in November instead of in the spring like other fruit trees. Small birds and small boys willingly eat the berries, which are too sour for adult palates.

The sitting room, with its two big windows looking out to the forest, is a bright room. Most of the wall space is taken up by my books. The rugs are worn and tattered—they have been with the house right from the beginning, I think—and I can't afford new ones.

On books and friends I spend my money;
For stones and bricks I haven't any.

Sir E, quite recovered from his recent illness, has gone down to Dehra again to attend to his farm and the demands of his farm workers. He should be back at the end of the month.

The brilliant blue-black of the whistling thrush shows up best when the sun is glinting off its back, but this seldom happens, because the bird likes to keep to the shade where it is almost black. Hopping about, it reminds me of Fred Astaire dancing in top hat and tails.

Now that it's getting hot, my small pool attracts a number of afternoon visitors—the mynas, babblers, a bulbul, a magpie. After their dip they perch in the cherry tree to dry themselves and I can watch them without getting up from my bed, where I take an afternoon siesta. I reserve the afternoons for doing nothing. 'Silence and non-action are the root of all things,' says the Tao. Especially on a drowsy afternoon.

But I haven't seen the whistling thrush for several days. Perhaps he is offended at having to share the pool which he was the first to discover. I haven't heard his song either, which probably means that he has moved down to the stream where it is cooler and shadier.

Prem's mother and younger sister come for a few days. His mother is a very quiet woman and doesn't say much even to her son. She is quite handsome, although she looks rather worn and tired, due probably to her recent illness.

His little sister, about four, is a friendly little gazelle; not in the least pretty, but lively and intelligent. She will have to stay here for at least six months to be properly treated for incipient tuberculosis. There is no treatment to be had in their village.

While I am resting, still exhausted from an attack of hill dysentery (who called this a health resort?), Sir E blows in, red-faced, as distressed as a stranded whale. His Gurkha servant has walked out, after quarrelling with his wife and mother-in-law, and has taken with him his twin sons (aged one and a half). I calm Sir E, tell him Trilok will be back in a day or two—he is probably trying to show how indispensable he is!

Sir E takes out a cigarette and strikes a match, and the entire matchbox flares up, burning a finger. Definitely not his day. I apply Burnol.

'It's all that damned girl's fault,' he says. 'She has a vile temper just like her mother. We were very wise not to marry, Ruskin.'

Wise or not, I seem to have acquired a family all the same.

※

Hundreds of white butterflies are flitting through the forest.

When Prem told his mother that I kept a human skull in my sitting room (as I have said earlier in the book, it was given to me by Anil), she told him not to spend too much time near it. If he did, he would be possessed by the spirit of the woman who had originally inhabited the skull.

But Prem, at the present time, is immune to spirits, having succumbed to the charms of his young wife who stays downstairs with his mother. They have only been married a few months. He leans over the balcony, chatting with her; advises her on how to keep the courtyard clean; then makes her a small broom from the twigs of a wild honeysuckle bush. She enjoys all the attention she is getting.

The sky is overcast this morning. Dust from the plains has formed a thick haze which hides the valley and the mountains. We are badly in need of rain. Down in the plains, over 200 people have died of heatstroke.

I haven't seen Bijju for some days, but this morning his sister, Binya, was out with the cows. What a sturdy little girl she is, and pretty, too. I will write a story about her.[*]

---

[*]This story was called 'The Blue Umbrella'.

'We'll take you to the pictures one day, Sir Edmund.'

'Yes, I must see one more picture before I die.'

So there comes a time when we start thinking in terms of the last picture, the last book, the last visit, the last party. But Sir E's remark is matter of fact. He is given to boredom but not to melancholy.

And he has a timeless quality. I have noticed this in other old people; they look more permanent than the young.

He sums it all up by saying, 'I don't mind being dead, but I shall miss being alive.'

A number of small birds are here to bathe and drink in the little pool beneath the cherry tree, hunting parties of tits—grey tits, red-headed tits and green-backed tits—and two delicate little willow warblers. They take turns in the pool. While the green-backs are taking a plunge, the red-heads wait patiently on the moss-covered rocks, coming down later to dip daintily at the edge of the pool; they don't like getting their feet wet! Finally, when they have all gone away, the whistling thrush arrives and indulges in an orgy of bathing, as he now has the entire pool to himself.

The babblers are adept at snapping up the little garden skinks that scuttle about in the leaves and grass. The skinks are quite brittle and are easily broken to pieces with a few hard raps of the beak. Then down they go! Babblers are also good at sifting through dead leaves and seizing upon various insects.

The honeybees push their way through the pursed lips of the antirrhinum and disappear completely. A few minutes later they stagger out again, bottoms first.

1 June

The dry spell continues. It is only before sunrise that there is any freshness in the air.

At dawn I said, 'Day, you will not begin without me.' I was

up with the whistling thrush at five. The cicadas were tuning up, the crickets were already in full cry, and the whistling thrush was calling most sweetly. As none of these songsters could be seen, it was as though the forest itself was singing.

Feeling the dawn wind stir, I was happy that I had met the day at its very beginning.

When the sun came up, the day became sultry and oppressive. I had to walk two miles to Ban Suman and back. There was no shade anywhere along the road. But we are equipped with legs for the purpose of walking. As more and more people grow dependent on their cars, a new species of humans will evolve. Around the turn of the twenty-second century, I can see legless humans being born. By then, of course, there will be flying wheelchairs.

A pall of dust hangs over the mountain.

Someone asked Sir E if he could shoot a bird on his land at Ramgarh. The man wanted the bird for dissection in a biology lab. Sir E refused. 'It's in the interests of science,' protested the man. 'Do you think a bird is better than a human?'

'Infinitely,' said Sir E. 'Infinitely better.'

He goes down today to pay his farmhands. He will return in a few days unless it gets cooler in Dehra. He complains of being very bored up here, for he can't get about, and in Dehra he has his Hillman. 'I'm *rotting* with boredom,' he says.

Vinod, I hear, is laid low with a fever—the result of a day's hard work. He is now in retirement for the rest of the season.

Walked five miles down the Tehri road to Suakholi, where I rested in a small tea shop, a loose stone structure with a tin roof held down by stones. It serves the bus passengers, mule drivers, milkmen and others who use this road.

I find a couple of mules tethered to a pine tree. The mule drivers, handsome men in tattered clothes, sit on a bench in the shade of the tree, drinking tea from brass tumblers. The shopkeeper, a man of indeterminate age—the cold dry winds from the mountain passes having crinkled his face like a walnut—greets me enthusiastically, as he always does. He even produces a chair, which looks like a survivor from the Savoy's 1890 ballroom. Fortunately, the Mussoorie antique dealers haven't seen it, or it would have been carried away long ago. In any case, the stuffing has come out of the seat. The shopkeeper apologizes for its condition, 'The rats were nesting in it.' And then, to reassure me, 'But they have gone now.'

Unlike the shopkeeper, the mule drivers have somewhere to go and something to deliver— sacks of potatoes. From Jaunpur to Jaunsar, the potato is probably the crop best suited to these stony, terraced fields. Oddly enough, it was introduced to the Himalayas by two Irishmen, Captain Young of Dehra and Mussoorie and Captain Kennedy of Simla, in the 1820s. The slopes of Young's house, Mullingar, were known as his Potato Farm. Looking up old books, I was surprised to learn that the potato wasn't known in India before the nineteenth century, and now it's an essential part of our diet in most parts of the country.

As the mule drivers lead their pack animals away, along the dusty road to Landour bazaar, I follow at a distance, singing 'Mule Train' in my best Nelson Eddy manner.*

A thunderstorm, followed by strong winds, brought down the temperature. That was yesterday. And today, 1 June, it is cloudy, cool, drizzling a little, almost monsoon weather; but it is still too early for the real monsoon.

The birds are enjoying the cool weather. The green-backed tits cool their bottoms in the rainwater pool. A king crow flashes past, winging through the air like an arrow. On the wing, it snaps up a hovering dragonfly. The mynas fetch crow feathers to line their nest in the eaves of the house. I am lying so still on the window seat that a tit alights on the sill within a few inches of my head. It snaps up a small dead moth before flying away.

---

*Not Nelson's song originally, but he sang it better than anyone else.

Sir E is back. He found it too hot in the valley. Even up here he has given up wearing a necktie. I'll have him wearing a kurta and pyjamas before long; the only sensible dress in summer.

At dusk I sit at the window and watch the trees and listen to the wind as it makes light conversation in the leafy tops of the maples. A large bat flits in and out of the trees. The sky is just light enough to enable me to see the bat and the outlines of the taller trees. Up on Landour hill, the lights are just beginning to come on. It is deliciously cool, eight o'clock, a perfect summer's evening. Prem is singing to himself in the kitchen. His wife and sister are chattering beneath the walnut tree. Down the hill, a kakar is barking, alarmed perhaps by the presence of a leopard. All the birds have gone to sleep for the night. Even the cicadas are strangely silent. The wind grows stronger and the tall maples bow before it; the maple moves its slender branches slowly from side to side, the oak moves its branches up and down. It is darker now; more lights on in Landour. The cry of the barking deer has grown fainter, more distant, and now I hear a cricket singing in the bushes. The stars are out, the wind grows chilly, it is time to close the window.

※

Bijju is very much an outdoor boy, even when he isn't grazing cows. He isn't very strong in the chest, but his legs are sturdy; he was having no difficulty in scaling the high retaining wall. He grinned down at me. He is rather like the whistling thrush—absent for days, then unexpectedly reappearing in the forest or on the hillside. Bijju sings too, although his voice is more vigorous than melodic.

And that reminds me of the story of the whistling thrush. The bird was once a village boy who tried very hard to play the flute in the same style as the god Krishna. When the god heard his favourite melody being plagiarized, he was furious and turned the unfortunate boy into a bird. The whistling thrush still tries to copy the divine melody, but somehow it always breaks off right in the middle of a stanza. There ought to be a moral here, especially in a land full of plagiarists. Or to be fair, I should say film-land...

The Whistler. This is my name for the youth who labours part-time in the school. He is something of a character—scatterbrained, carefree, easy-going. He is always whistling—loudly and quite tunefully (this time a bird turned into a boy?) so that you know when he's coming round a bend or through the trees, and even when it's dark you know who it is. He's usually out quite late, because he spends all his money at the pictures. He has three sisters, and they and the mother are all working as maids or ayahs, and as they are quite indulgent to him (the only brother) he doesn't have to work too hard. His shoes are always torn, even though his clothes look new.

He has a reputation for being a waster, but he returned the few rupees he borrowed from me last month. I suppose a youth who is always singing and whistling on the roads gives everyone the impression that he has nothing to do from morn till night, unlike that jolly Miller of Dee who worked *and* sang the whole day through. (I know one man who forbids his children from singing in the home.)

But back to the Whistler, he is really quite enterprising. The other day he asked me for one of my books, and as I knew he hadn't squandered too many years in school, I gave him an easy Hindi translation of one of my children's books. But it was the paper he valued, not the words. He flogged it to the bania's small son, who took it apart and converted the large pages into envelopes, which were then used for selling gram and peanuts. In India, it doesn't take long for anything to be recycled. On the way home, I saw a couple of customers throwing their empty packets away, and these were promptly consumed by a stray cow. There went my beautiful story!

Is there a lesson to be learnt from this? Yes. Don't throw

away complimentaries.

It rained all night, and the morning is cool and fresh. Parrots are on the wing. I feel like tap-dancing like Gene Kelly, but you can't tap dance on a hillside, you'd break an ankle. Only the roads (and not all of them) are suitable for a song-and-dance act, and no doubt the Whistler will oblige before long. At forty, I must refrain from being too frisky and boyish. But I'll do a reel in the garden when no one is looking.

24 June

The first day of monsoon mist. And it's strange how all the birds fall silent as the mist comes climbing up the hill. Perhaps that's what makes the mist so melancholy; not only does it conceal the hills, it blankets them in silence too. Only an hour ago the trees were ringing with birdsong. And now the forest is deathly still, as though it were midnight.

Through the mist Bijju is calling to his sister. I can hear him running about on the hillside but I cannot see him.

Feeling sorry for Sir E (or maybe for myself), I walked over to see him. The door was closed, so I looked in at the French window (nothing could be more *English* than a French window, and no Agatha Christie mystery would be complete without one), and I saw him sleeping in his chair with his chin on his chest. There was no dagger sticking out of his back, only a bit of stuffing from his old coat. My footsteps on the gravel woke him, and he got up and opened the door for me. He said he felt a bit tipsy; he had taken his usual peg, but thought the quality of whisky varied from bottle to bottle, and wished he could lay his hands on a bottle of Scotch or even Irish. He could only offer me an Uttar Pradesh brand. I said I'd given up drinking, and this pleased him because in truth he hates anyone drinking his whisky; said he might give it up himself, it 'cost too damn much!' I told him it would be unwise to give up drinking at this stage of his life. As he had reached the age of eighty-six on two pegs a day, he was obviously thriving on it. Giving it up now would only play havoc with the orderly working of his system. I'd given it up in order to help an alcoholic friend abstain, and also because I wanted to give up *something*, and strong drink seemed the easiest thing to do without.

A cicada starts up in the tree nearest my window seat. What has he been doing all these weeks, and why does he choose this particular evening to play the fiddle so loudly? The cicadas are late this year, the monsoon has been late. But soon the forest will be ringing with the sound of the cicadas—an orchestra constantly tuning up but never quite getting into tune—and the sound of the birds will be pushed into the background.

Outside the front door I found an elegant young praying mantis reclining on a leaf of the honeysuckle creeper. I say young because he hadn't grown to his full size, and was that very tender pale green which is the colour of a young mantis. They are light brown to begin with, like dry twigs, but as they grow older and the monsoon foliage becomes greener, they too change, and by mid-August they are dark green.

❦

As though to make up for lost time, the monsoon rains are now here with a vengeance. It has been pouring all day, and already the roof is leaking. But nothing dampens Prem's spirits. He is still singing love songs in the kitchen.

Kailash, whom I have known for a couple of weeks, asks me for twenty-five rupees.

'What do you need it for?' I ask.

'It's for my Sanskrit teacher,' he says. 'I have failed in Sanskrit but if I give the teacher twenty-five rupees he'll alter my marks. You see, I've passed in all the other subjects, but if I fail in Sanskrit I'll fail the entire exams and remain a pre-Inter student for another year.'

I took a little time to digest this information and ponder

on the pitfalls of the examination system.

'He must be failing a lot of boys,' I said. 'Twenty-five rupees each! Are there many others?'

'Some. But he dare not fail the good ones. They can ask for a re-check. It's the borderline cases like me who give him a chance to make money.'

This placed me in a quandary. Should I yield to the evils of the examination system and provide the money for pass-marks? Or should I adopt a high moral stance and allow the boy to fail?

Whatever the evils of the exam system, they are not the fault of the student. And either way he isn't going to turn into a great Sanskrit scholar. So why be a hypocrite? I gave him the money.

Kailash slogs in his uncle's orchard all morning, gets a midday meal (no breakfast), and hasn't any shoes. And yet his uncle, a member of one of Garhwal's well-known upper caste families, is a wealthy man.

Kailash tells me he will return to his village once he knows his result. According to him, his uncle is such a miser that at mealtimes he pauses before each mouthful, wondering, 'Ought I to eat it? Or should I keep it for tomorrow?'

I am visited by another kind of student, a small girl from one of the private schools. Her mother has brought her to me for my autograph.

'She studies your book in Class 6,' I was informed.

'And what book is that?' I asked the little girl.

'*Tom Sawyer*,' she replied promptly. So I signed for Mark Twain.

When a small storeroom collapsed during the last heavy rains, I was forced to rescue a couple of old packing cases that had been left there for three or four years—since my arrival here, in fact. The contents were well-soaked and most of it had to be thrown away—old manuscripts that had been obliterated, negatives that had got stuck together, gramophone records that had taken on strange shapes (dear 'Ink Spots', how will I ever listen to you again?*)... Unlike most writers, I have no compunction about throwing away work that hasn't quite come off, and I am sure there are a few critics who would prefer that I throw away the lot! Sentimental rubbish, no doubt. Well, we can't please everyone; and we can't preserve everything either. Time and the elements will take their toll.

But a couple of old diaries, kept in exercise books almost twenty years ago, had managed to survive the rain, and I put them out in the sun to dry, and then, almost unwillingly, started browsing through them, It was instructive, and sometimes a little disconcerting, to discover the sort of person I had been in my twenties. In some ways, no different from what I am today. In other ways, radically different. A diary is a useful tool for self-examination, particularly if both diary and diarist are still around after some years.

One particular entry caught my eye, and I reproduce it here without any alteration, because it represented my credo as a young writer, and it set me wondering if I had lived up to my own expectations. (Nobody else had any expectations of me!)

The entry was made on 19 January 1958, when I was living on my own in Dehradun:

> The things I do best are those things I do on my own, alone, of my own accord, without the advice or approval of others. Once I start doing what other people tell me to do, both my character and creativity take a dip. It is when I strike out on my own that I succeed best.
>
> There was a time when I was much younger and poorer than I am now. I have been over a year in Jersey, in the Channel Islands; I was unhappy, and the atmosphere in which I was writing was one of discouragement and disapproval. And that was why I wrote so well—because I was defiant! That was why I finished the only book I have finished so

---

*This was before the advent of audiotapes.

far. I had to prove to myself that I could do it.

One night I was walking alone along the beach. There was a strong wind blowing, dashing the salt spray in my face, and the sea was crashing against the St Helier rocks. I told myself; I will go to London; I will take up a job; I will finish my book; I will find a publisher; I will save money and I will return to India, because I can be happier there than here.

And that was just what I did.

I had guts then.

What's more, I had an end in view.

The writing itself is not enough for me. Success and money are not enough. I had a little of both recently[*], but they did not help me do anything wonderful. I must have something to write for, just as I must have something to live for. And that's something I have yet to find.

There was more in that vein, but I give this excerpt as an example of a young man's determination to be a writer in what were then adverse circumstances. Thirty-five years later, I'm still trying.

27 June

The rains have heralded the arrival of some seasonal visitors—a leopard, and several thousand leeches.

Yesterday afternoon the leopard lifted a dog from near the servants' quarters below the school. In the evening it attacked one of Bijju's cows but fled at the approach of Bijju's mother, who came screaming imprecations.

As for the leeches, I shall soon get used to a little bloodletting every day. Bijju's mother sat down in the shrubbery to relieve herself, and later discovered two fat black leeches feeding on her fair round bottom. I told her she could use one of the spare

---

[*]When *The Room on the Roof* was published (1956).

bathrooms downstairs. But she prefers the wide, open spaces.

Other new arrivals are the scarlet minivets (the females are yellow), flitting silently among the leaves like brilliant jewels. No matter how leafy the trees, these brightly coloured birds cannot conceal themselves, although, by remaining absolutely silent, they sometimes contrive to go unnoticed. Along came a pair of drongos, unnecessarily aggressive, chasing the minivets away.

A creeper moves rapidly up the trunk of the oak tree, snapping up insects all the way. Now that the rains are here, there is no dearth of food for the insectivorous birds.

In spite of there being water in several places, the whistling thrush still comes to my pool. He, at least, is a permanent resident.

※

Kailash has a round, cheerful face, only slightly marred by a swivel eye. His hair comes down over his forehead, hiding a deep scar. He is short, but quite compact and energetic. He chatters a good deal but in a general sort of way, and a response isn't obligatory.

It's quite possible that he will go away as soon as he gets his exam results. He's fed up with being the Cinderella of his uncle's house. He tells of how his miserly uncle went to see a rather permissive film, and was very shocked and wanted to walk out, but couldn't bear the thought of losing his ticket money; so he sat through the film with his eyes closed.

Sir E departed for Dehra with his large retinue of servants and their dependents, all of whom would have done justice to an eighteenth-century-nawab. 'I am at the mercy of my servants,' he told me the other day.

But he had placed himself at their mercy long ago, by setting himself up as a country squire surrounded by 'faithful retainers'—all of whom received generous salaries but did little or no work. If he sold his white elephant of a farm, he'd be quite comfortable with one servant.

'I'll probably come up in September, after the rains,' he said.

'If I live that long… I'm just living day to day.'

'So am I,' I told him. 'It's the best way to live.'

A couple of days passed before Kailash came to see me. I was beginning to wonder if he'd come again. Apparently the teacher had at first proved elusive, but the deed was done, and Kailash passed with the marks he needed. Ironically, his uncle was so impressed that he is now urging the boy to remain with him and complete the Intermediate exam.

'I must write a story about your uncle,' I remark.

'Don't give him a story', says Kailash. 'A short note will do.'

Now that Prem is preoccupied with his wife, and the house is at the mercy of uninvited visitors, I stay out most of the time, and these days Kailash is my only companion. Yesterday, we took Camel's Back Road, past the cemetery. He chatters away, and I can listen if I want to, or think or other things if I don't want to listen; apparently it makes no difference to him. He is a cheerful soul, with an infectious laugh. He walks with a slight swagger, or roll. He says he doesn't mind staying here now that he has me for a friend; that he can put up with two sour uncles as long as he knows I'm around. I suppose he's quite capable of pulling a fast one on his uncle, but all the same, I find myself liking him.

❊

Moody. And when I'm moody I'm bad.

Prem says, 'It is easier to please god than it is to please you.'

'But god is easily pleased,' I respond. 'God makes absolutely no demands on us. We just imagine them.'

The eyes.

Prem's eyes have great gentleness in them.

His wife's eyes are round and mischievous and suggestive…

Suggestive enough to invite the attention of a mischievous or malignant spirit.

At about two in the morning I am awakened by Prem's shouts, muffled by rain. Shouting back that I am on my way, for it is obviously an emergency, I leap out of bed, grab an umbrella, dash outside and then down the stairs to his room. His wife is sobbing in bed. Whatever had possessed her has now gone away, and the crying is due more to Prem's ministrations—he exorcizes the ghost by thumping her on the head—than to the 'possession' itself. But there is no doubt that she is subject to hallucinatory or subconscious actions. It is not simply a hysterical fit. She walks in her sleep, moves restlessly from door to window, holds conversations with an invisible presence, and resists all efforts to bring her back to reality. When she comes out of the trance, she is quite normal.

This sort of thing is apparently quite common in the hills, where people believe it to be a ghost taking temporary possession of a human mind. It's happened to Prem's wife before, and it also happens to her brother, so it seems to run in the family. It never happens to Prem, who deeply resents the interruption to his sleep.

I calm the girl and then make them bring their bedding upstairs. I give her a sleeping tablet and she is soon fast asleep.

During a lull in the rain, I hear a most hideous sound coming from the forest—a maniacal shrieking, followed by a mournful hooting. But Prem and his wife sleep through it all. The rain starts again, and the shrieking stops. Perhaps, it's a hyena. Perhaps, something else.

A morning of bright sunshine, and the whistling thrush welcomes it with a burst of song. Where do the birds shelter when it rains? How does that frail butterfly survive the battering of strong winds and heavy raindrops? How do the snakes manage in their flooded holes?

I saw a bright green snake sunning itself on some rocks; no doubt waiting for its hole to dry out.

※

In my vagrant days, ten to fifteen years ago (long before the hippies made vagrancy commonplace), I was a great frequenter of tea shops, those dingy little shacks with a table and three chairs, a grimy tea kettle, and a cracked gramophone. Tea shops haven't changed much, and once again I find myself lingering in them, sometimes in company with Kailash, who, although he doesn't eat much, drinks a lot of tea.

One can sit all day in a tea shop and watch the world go by. Amazing the number of people who actually do this! And not all of them unemployed. The tea shop near the clock tower is ideal for this purpose. It is a busy part of the bazaar but the tea shop, though small, is gloomy within, and one can loll about unseen, observing everyone who passes by a few feet away in the sunlit (or rain-spattered) street. The tea itself is indifferent, the buns are stale, the boiled eggs have been peppered too liberally. Kailash is unusually quiet; there is no one else in the shop. People who stop me on the road pass by without glancing into the murky interior. This is the ideal place; not as noble as my window opening into the trees, but familiar, reminiscent of days gone by in Dehra, when cares sat lightly upon me simply because I did not care at all. And now perhaps I have begun to care too much.

I gave Bijju a cake. He licked all the icing off it, only then did he eat the rest.

❀

It was a dark windy corner in Landour bazaar, but I always found the old man there, hunched up by the charcoal fire on which he roasted his peanuts. He'd been there for as long as I could remember, and he could be seen at almost any hour of the day or night. Summer or winter, he stayed close to his fire.

He was probably quite tall, but we never saw him standing. One judged his height from his long, loose limbs. He was very thin, and the high cheekbones added to the tautness of his tightly stretched skin.

His peanuts were always fresh, crisp and hot. They were popular with the small boys who had a few paise to spend on their way to and from school, and with the patrons of the cinemas, many of whom made straight for the windy corner during intervals or when the show was over. On cold winter evenings, or misty monsoon days, there was always a demand for the old man's peanuts.

No one knew his name. No one had ever thought of asking him for it. One just took him for granted. He was as fixed a landmark as a clock tower or the old cherry tree that grew crookedly from the hillside. The tree was always being lopped; the clock often stopped. The peanut vendor seemed less perishable than the trees, more dependable than the clock.

He had no family, but in a way all the world was his family, because he was in continuous contact with people. And yet he was a remote sort of being; always polite, even to children, but never familiar. There is a distinction to be made between aloneness and loneliness. The peanut vendor was seldom alone; but he must have been lonely.

Summer nights he rolled himself up in a thin blanket and slept on the ground, beside the dying embers of his fire. During the winter he waited until the last show was over, before retiring to the rickshaw-coolies' shed where there was some protection from the biting wind.

Did he enjoy being alive? I wonder now. He was not a joyful person; but then, neither was he miserable. I should think he was genuine stoic, one of those who do not attach overmuch importance to themselves, who are emotionally uninvolved, content with their limitations, their dark corners. I wanted to get to know the old man better, to sound him out on the immense questions involved in roasting peanuts all his life; but it's too late now. The last time I visited the bazaar the dark corner was deserted. The old man had vanished; the coolies had carried him down to the cremation ground.

'He died in his sleep,' said the tea shop owner. 'He was very old.'

Very old. Sufficient reason to die.

But that corner is very empty, very dark, and whenever I pass it I am haunted by visions of the old peanut vendor, troubled by the questions I failed to ask; and I wonder if he was really as indifferent to life as he appeared to be.

❧

Prem brought his wife some of her favourite mangoes. This afternoon he took her into my room so that she could listen to the radio. They both fell asleep at opposite ends of the bed; are still asleep as I write this in the next room, at my window. If I curled up a little, I could fall asleep here on the window seat. Nothing would induce me to disturb those innocents; they look far too blissful in their slumbers.

❧

Kailash and I are caught in a storm and it's by far the worst storm of the year. To make matters worse, there is absolutely no shelter for a mile along the main road from the town. It was fierce, lashing rain, quite cold, whipping along on the wind from all angles. The road was soon a torrent of muddy water, as earth and stones came rushing down the hillsides. Our one umbrella was useless and was very nearly blown away. The cardboard carton in which we were carrying vegetables was soon reduced to pulp. We broke into a run, although we could hardly see our way. There were blinding flashes of lightning—is an umbrella a good or bad conductor of electricity? Kailash sees humour in these situations and was in peals of laughter all the way home, even when we slid into a ditch.

He takes my hand and holds it between his hands. He is happy. He got his self-confidence back, and can now deal with his uncles and Sanskrit teachers.

In the morning I work on a story. There is a dove cooing in the garden. Now it is very quiet, the only sound is the distant tapping of a woodpecker. The trees are muffled in ferns and creepers. It is mid-monsoon.

Kailash, his hair falling in an untidy mop across his forehead, drags me out of the house and over the wet green grass on the hillside.

I protest that I do not like leeches, so we make for the high rocks. He laughs, talks, chuckles, and when he grins his large front teeth make him look like a 1940s Mickey Rooney. When he looks sullen (this happens when he talks about his uncle), he looks Brando-ish. He has the gift of being able to convey his effervescence to me. Am I, at my age, too old to be gambolling about on the hill slopes like a young colt? (Am I, sobering thought, going to be a character of enforced youthfulness like the man on the boat in *Death in Venice*? Well, better that than Gissing's hero of *New Grub Street* who's old at forty.) If I am fit enough to gambol, then I must gambol. If I can still climb a tree, then I must climb trees, instead of just watching them from my window. I was in such high spirits yesterday that I kept playing the clown, and I haven't done this in years. To walk in the rain was fun, and to get wet was fun, and to fall down was fun, and to get hurt was fun.

'Will it last?' asks Kailash.

'This feeling of love between us?'

'*This* won't last. Not in this way. But if something *like* it lasts, we should be happy.'

❦

Prem is happy, laughing, giggling all the time. Sometimes it is a little annoying for me, because he is obviously unaware of what is happening around him—such as the fact that part of the roof blew away in the storm—but I am a good Taoist, I say nothing, I wait for the right moment! Besides, it's a crime to interfere with anyone's happiness.

Prem notices the roof is missing and scolds his wife for seeing too many pictures. 'She's seen ten pictures in two months.

More than she'd seen in her whole life, before coming here.' She pulls a face. Says Prem, 'My grandfather will be here any day to take her home.'

'Then she can see pictures with your grandfather,' I venture. 'While we can repair the roof.'

'I wouldn't go anywhere with that old man,' she says.

'Don't speak like that of my grandfather. Do you want a beating? Look at Binya'—we all look at Binya, who is perched very prettily on the wall—'she hasn't seen more than two pictures in her life!'

'I'll take her to the pictures,' I offer.

Binya gives me a radiant smile. She'd love to go to the pictures, but her mother won't allow it.

Prem relents and takes his wife to the pictures.

Binya's mother has a bad attack of hiccups. Serves her right, for stealing my walnuts and not letting me take Binya to the pictures.

In the evening I find Prem teaching his wife the alphabet, using the lichen door as a blackboard. It is covered with chalk marks. Love is teaching your wife to read and write!

❀

These entries were made in 1973, twenty years ago.

The following year I did not keep a journal, but these are some of the things that happened:

Sir E had a stroke and, like a stranded whale, finally heaved his last breath. According to his wishes, he was cremated on his farm near Dehra.

To Prem and Chandra was born a son, Rakesh, who immediately stole my heart—and gave me many a sleepless night, for as a baby he cried lustily.

Kailash went into the army and disappeared from my life, as we from his uncle's.

Bijju and Binya were to remain a part of the hillside for several years.

UPON AN OLD WALL DREAMING

It is time to confess that at least half of my life has been spent in idleness. My old school would not be proud of me. Nor would my Aunt Muriel.

'You spend most of your time sitting on that wall, doing nothing,' scolded Aunt Muriel, when I was seven or eight. 'Are you *thinking* about something?'

'No, Aunt Muriel.'

'Are you *dreaming*?'

'I'm awake!'

'Then what on earth are you doing there?'

'Nothing, Aunt Muriel.'

'He'll come to no good,' she warned the world at large. 'He'll spend all his life sitting on walls, doing nothing.'

And how right she proved to be! Sometimes I bestir myself, and bang out a few sentences on my old typewriter, but most of the time I'm still sitting on the wall, preferably in the winter sunshine. Thinking? Not very deeply. Dreaming? But I've grown too old to dream. Meditation, perhaps. That's been fashionable for some time. But it isn't that either. Contemplation might come closer to the mark.

Was I born with a silver spoon in my mouth that I could afford to sit in the sun for hours, doing nothing? Far from it; I was born poor and remained poor, as far as worldly riches went. But one has to eat and pay the rent. And there have been others to feed too. So I have to admit that between long bouts of idleness there have been short bursts of creativity. My typewriter, after more than thirty years of loyal service, has finally collapsed, proof enough that it has not lain idle all this time.

Sitting on walls, apparently doing nothing, has always been my favourite form of inactivity. But for these walls, and the many idle hours I have spent upon them, I would not have written even a fraction of the hundreds of stories, essays and other diversions that have been banged out on the typewriter over the years. It is not the walls themselves that set me off or give me ideas, but a personal view of the world that I receive from sitting there.

Creative idleness, you could call it. A receptivity to the world around me—the breeze, the warmth of the old stone, the lizard on the rock, a raindrop on a blade of grass—these and other impressions impinge upon me as I sit in that passive, benign condition that makes people smile tolerantly at me as they pass. 'Eccentric writer' they remark to each other, as they drive on, hurrying in a heat of hope, towards the pot of gold at the end of their personal rainbows.

It's true that I am eccentric in many ways, and old walls bring out the essence of my eccentricity.

I do not have a garden wall. This shaky, tumbledown house in the hills is perched directly above a motorable road, making me both accessible and vulnerable to casual callers of all kinds—inquisitive tourists, local busybodies, schoolgirls with their poems, hawkers selling candyfloss, itinerant sadhus, scrap merchants, potential Nobel Prize winners...

To escape them, and to set my thoughts in order, I walk a little way up the road, cross it, and sit down on a parapet wall overlooking the Woodstock spur. Here, partially shaded by an overhanging oak, I am usually left alone. I look suitably down and out, shabbily dressed, a complete nonentity—not the sort of person you would want to be seen talking to!

Stray dogs sometimes join me here. Having been a stray dog myself at various periods of my life, I can empathize with these friendly vagabonds of the road. Far more intelligent than your inbred Pom or peke, they let me know by their silent companionship that they are on the same wavelength. They sport about on the road, but they do not yap at all and sundry.

Left to myself on the wall, I am soon in the throes of composing a story or poem. I do not write it down—that can be done later—I just work it out in my mind, memorize my words, so to speak, and keep them stored up for my next writing session.

Occasionally a car will stop, and someone I know will stick his head out and say, 'No work today, Mr Bond? How I envy you! Not a care in the world!'

I travel back in time some fifty years ago to Aunt Muriel asking me the same question. The years melt away, and I am a child again, sitting on the garden wall, doing nothing.

'Don't you get bored sitting there?' asks the latest passing motorist, who has one of those half-beards which are in vogue with TV news readers. 'What are you doing?'

'Nothing, Aunty,' I reply.

He gives me a long hard stare.

'You must be dreaming. Don't you recognize me?'

'Yes, Aunt Muriel.'

He shakes his head sadly, steps on the gas, and goes roaring up the hill in a cloud of dust.

'Poor old Bond,' he tells his friends over evening cocktails. 'Must be going round the bend. This morning he called me Aunty.'

STORIES TO TELL

India is a land of festivals, and during the last three or four years we have added one more festival to our calendar of delights—the literary festival.

Kolkata has always had its book fairs and literary occasions, but the 'lit fest' as we know it—the coming together of writers and book lovers—received an impetus a few years ago in Jaipur and has since spread to almost every town and city in a land hungering for intellectual nourishment: Pune, Goa, Bhubaneswar, Agra, Allahabad, Travancore, Kasauli, Mussoorie, Patna, not to mention our major cities. And now even schools and other institutions are conducting their own festivals; perhaps we had a surfeit of technological nourishment and are looking for something a little more creative and personal.

All the literary activity has come about because in recent years large numbers of Indian writers have been making it big on the national and international scene. And in this era of television and the Internet, successful writers soon become celebrities.

That means writing has at last become fashionable. Fame is the spur!

When I was a boy with literary ambitions I did dream of becoming a famous writer one day. What are dreams for, after all? Even if we fail, we can still dream. They keep us hoping and striving—and dreaming!

In those far-off days there were no literary festivals. Book launches were rare. Authors were read, seldom heard or seen. P. G. Wodehouse tells us of how at a literary get-together, his hostess came up to him and said, 'So good of you to come. I've always wanted to meet Edgar Wallace!'

My literary icons were Somerset Maugham, Hugh Walpole, J. B. Priestley, Graham Greene, H. E. Bates, and of course P. G. Wodehouse. I read almost everything they wrote. But they were 'invisible' authors. Their names may have been household words, but you seldom saw them in person. Sometimes a smudgy black-and-white photograph appeared on the back cover of a book, but that was all. A successful playwright such as J. M. Barrie might take a bow at the end of the opening night of *Peter Pan*, and that was it. He would then return to his eyrie to write another play or novel. And it was the same with Maugham who, because of his stammer, hated making public appearances.

In 1953, when I was living and working in London—just nineteen years old—a young producer invited me to give a talk on the BBC's Home Service (those were radio days) on what it was like to grow up in India before and after Independence. While I was waiting for my turn in the studio, a tall good-looking man of about forty entered the small waiting room and sat down beside me. We exchanged pleasantries, mostly about the weather and the coming Coronation (nothing very intellectual, I'm afraid) and then he got up and left the room. My producer came in just then and said, 'I see you have met Graham Greene. He was here for a book programme.'

So the stranger had been Graham Greene, then probably at the height of his fame as a novelist. He had recently written the script for the film *The Third Man*, which had been having a successful run in the West End cinemas. I had read several of his books—*Brighton Rock*, *Stamboul Train*, *The Confidential Agent*—but I hadn't recognized him!

How wonderful to be anonymous!

Had Graham Greene been one of the stars in his film, he would have been recognized immediately. But one of the charms of being an author was that you could be 'invisible'—just another wayfarer roaming the streets in search of a story.

In search of a story...

For that, in a way, is what writing is all about. Looking for a story—and telling it.

When I was starting out as a writer, an author was someone who'd had a book published. Until that happened, you were just a writer! I remember when my first novel was finally accepted (after submitting three rewrites) my editor and publisher, Diana Athill, took me out to dinner and said, 'Well, Ruskin, you are finally an author!'

Diana Athill was then a young partner in the firm of André Deutsch. She was the first to publish V. S. Naipaul, Jack Kerouac, and other rising stars in the literary firmament. Her book about authors and publishers, called *Stet*, should be read by everyone who cares about the written world.

It was 1955, I was twenty-one, and my first book was about to be published. After a few years in London and the Channel Islands, I was on my way home to India. In many ways I was still a boy, with a boy's dreams. Thanks to all the great books I had read, I could write fluently and in a style of my own. But would writing sustain me?

Well, it did—but only just...

Those early years of freelancing in the India of the 1950s, 60s and 70s weren't easy, partly because good publishers were thin on the ground. But I was determined to make a living from my writing, and I was determined to do it here. The stories, the essays, the poems kept coming, and so, finally, did the publishers.

Sixty years after my first book, *The Room on the Roof,* was published, I am still scribbling away, still trying to be a better writer. Hundreds of stories have been told, but there are still stories to tell, for stories of love and childhood and kindness have no endings.

AND SUDDENLY IT'S SUMMER

The first of May, and suddenly it's summer. The potted plants cry out for water, and I give them whatever is in the tap. Most of it goes into the pudina patch. Pudina needs lots of water. And it's a healthy crop of pudina; enough to give us pudina chutney every day until we're sick of it. But I don't get sick of pudina chutney. It goes well with almost anything. I like it best on a hot buttered piece of toast.

Most of the trees are now in new leaf. Flowering candelabras hang from the chestnut trees. Cicadas sing in the oak trees.

Here comes a big fat bumblebee, sailing through my open window. I'm a little wary of bees, having been stung a few times. But as Granny used to say, 'Bee venom is good for you. Beekeepers always live to a good age.' Happy birthday, beekeepers! Long life to you! I'll stick to ladybirds. Plenty of them this year, and they don't bite or sting.

The moths arrive at dusk, attracted by the light in my room. Almost swallowed one yesterday. Must learn to keep my mouth shut. Moths taste like mud, in case you don't know. I remember seeing a ghazal singer swallow a moth while he was in the middle of a performance. It affected him very badly. Never again did he sing with the same freedom and abandon; always expecting some winged insect to fly into his open mouth and interfere with his vocal chords.

In India, there are many people, but even more insects—flies, mosquitoes, ants, bugs of all kinds. I have seen a famous wicketkeeper drop a catch because a fly was buzzing around in his helmet. And a great batsman being bowled out because a red ant had got into his protective box and bitten him at a crucial moment. Matches have been won and lost due to the prevalence of cricket-loving sandflies. And match-fixers can do nothing about insects.

Wars, too, have been won and lost because of them. When Alexander invaded India he did not know what he was letting himself in for. Summer arrived, and he was stranded in the Sind Desert. After being stung by scorpions and attacked by swarms of mosquitoes, he decided to go no further and made a tactical retreat to cooler climes.

And so summer is here again, with its millions of insects, some benevolent, some malevolent.

There's a big fat spider on my wall. Technically, spiders aren't insects, having two legs too many, and most of them are pretty harmless, although the females do tend to murder their husbands at the first opportunity.

It is said that when a spider runs up a wall it's a sign that rain is coming. When it runs down a wall, an earthquake is in the offing.

This particular spider, is very still and has a contented look about it, which probably means she has just feasted on her mate.

EPILOGUE

Time, You Old Gypsy Man

About six months ago some enthusiastic youngsters stuck several election posters on the wall opposite this building. I see them every morning from my window. I can't help looking at them—they are there right in front of me, inviting me to vote for the candidate whose well-groomed but expressionless visage greets me every morning along with the rising sun and the song of the whistling thrush.

I have no idea if the gentleman on the poster won or lost his election; it doesn't seem to matter. Sooner or later winners become losers and losers, winners. His rival in a companion poster looks equally confident, rather similar in looks, and I presume one of them now occupies a seat of importance in the local municipality.

But it is the posters themselves that fascinate me. Wind and weather have brought about a general deterioration in the material. One poster hangs loose, another is in shreds. Here and there bits of paper still adhere to the wall. A portion of a face can just be made out. Paan juice decorates a faded suit and tie. Every day there is a noticeable deterioration in these remnants of human endeavour. And in a way they mirror our own lives, although we take a little longer to lose our sheen, our polish.

I look at that poster and wonder, is this what has been happening to me over the years? Or do I resemble the portrait of Dorian Gray, gathering decay and corruption while the subject of the portrait remains forever youthful?

Something of both, perhaps.

But I am glad I've never been a poster boy. Celebrities come and go, and the years take their toll, so that the beautiful stars of yesteryear are barely recognizable when they advance into their sixties and seventies; for they are haunted by the images of their youth and the near-perfection of a physique as yet untouched by time.

> Time, you old gypsy man,
> Will you not stay,
> Put up your caravan
> Just for one day?

But Time and the caravan must trundle along, oblivious to our attempts to halt its inevitable journey towards some distant goal as yet unknown to us. For although the leaf decays, the seed and the leaf-mould combine to create new life, new beauty. And the poem itself survives. At least this one does.

Ralph Hodgson must have written hundreds of poems, but this is the one that has come down to us. I read it when I was a boy, and I read it again today, at the age of eighty-one. The caravan has moved on, leaving a little poem behind.

And as I sit here, watching the clouds go by, I think of all the hundreds of poems and stories that I have put to paper, and whether it matters if not even one of them survives my passing. For like the poster on the wall, the last shreds will soon be blown away.

And one day the road and the wall and the building will be gone. And then someday the mountain could change its shape. But the clouds will still roll by, and the wind and the rain will sing. And they will be the poem of all our days.

Ruskin Bond
25 December 2015

ACKNOWLEDGEMENTS

Almost all my early stories, novellas and essays made their first appearance in different periodicals and anthologies, both Indian and international. I would like to acknowledge these publications in the order in which the stories in this book are published. If a piece is appearing in the book for the first time I have not mentioned it in the acknowledgements below.

'Bus Stop, Pipalnagar': *The Night Train at Deoli and Other Stories*, Penguin India; 'A Face in the Dark': the *Illustrated Weekly of India*; 'My Father's Trees in Dehra': *Dust on the Mountain*, Penguin India; 'A Case for Inspector Lal': *The Writer on the Hill*, Rupa Publications India; 'The Thief's Story': the *Illustrated Weekly of India*; 'The Fight': *The Road to the Bazaar*, Rupa Publications India; 'Fairy Glen Palace': *Tales of Fosterganj*, Aleph Book Company; 'The Last Tiger': the *Illustrated Weekly of India*; 'Tiger in the Cemetery': *A Handful of Nuts*, Penguin India; 'Mrs Roberts': *Tehelka*; 'Life at My Own Pace': *The Heritage*; 'A Good Philosophy': *Deccan Herald*; 'Great Trees of Garhwal': the *Christian Science Monitor*; 'A Night Walk Home': *The Statesman*; 'Birdsong in the Hills', 'Once Upon a Mountain Time: the *Christian Science Monitor*; 'Upon an Old Wall Dreaming': *Deccan Herald*.

R. B.